HOW SHOULD A PERSON BE?

HOW SHOULD

A PERSON BE?

SHEILA HETI

Harvill Secker

LONDON

Published by Harvill Secker 2013

2 4 6 8 10 9 7 5 3

Copyright © 2012 by Sheila Heti
Originally published in a slightly different form in
Canada in 2010 by House of Anansi Press, Inc.

Sheila Heti has asserted her right under the Copyright,

Desig   work

Addresses fo   be found at:

A CIP catalogue record for this book is available from the British Library

ISBN 9781846557545

"James Joyce," from Matt Cook's *In the Small of My Backyard* (San Francisco:
Manic D Press, 2002), was used with permission from the author and publisher.

Ideas about the *puer aeternus* come from Ann Yeoman's *Now or Neverland*
(Toronto: Inner City Books, 1999) and Marie-Louise von Franz's *The Problem of the
Puer Aeternus* (Toronto: Inner City Books, 2000).

Northrop Frye's writing about Milton helped. So did many other texts.

The author acknowledges the support of the Corporation of Yaddo,
Fundación Valparaiso, and Santa Maddalena.

"Magic Penny" (Love Is Something), Words & Music by Malvina Reynolds, © Copyright 1955
MCA Northern Music Company Incorporated. Universal/MCA Music Limited.
All Rights Reserved. International Copyright Secured.

The Random House Group Limited supports The Forest Stewardship
Council® (FSC®), the leading international forest-certification organisation.
Our books carrying the FSC label are printed on FSC®-certified paper.
FSC is the only forest-certification scheme supported by the leading
environmental organisations, including Greenpeace. Our
paper procurement policy can be found at
www.randomhouse.co.uk/environment

Printed and bound in Great Britain by Clays Ltd, St Ives PLC

for Margaux

HOW SHOULD A PERSON BE?

PROLOGUE

How should a person be?

For years and years I asked it of everyone I met. I was always watching to see what they were going to do in any situation, so I could do it too. I was always listening to their answers, so if I liked them, I could make them my answers too. I noticed the way people dressed, the way they treated their lovers—in everyone, there was something to envy. You can admire anyone for being themselves. It's hard not to, when everyone's so good at it. But when you think of them all together like that, how can you choose? How can you say, *I'd rather be responsible like Misha than irresponsible like Margaux*? Responsibility looks so good on Misha, and irresponsibility looks so good on Margaux. How could I know which would look best on me?

I admired all the great personalities down through time,

like Andy Warhol and Oscar Wilde. They seemed to be so perfectly themselves in every way. I didn't think, *Those are great souls*, but I did think, *Those are some great personalities for our age.* Charles Darwin, Albert Einstein—they *did* things, but they *were* things.

I know that personality is just an invention of the news media. I know that character exists from the outside alone. I know that inside the body there's just temperature. So how do you build your soul? At a certain point, I know, you have to forget about your soul and just do the work you're required to do. To go on and on about your soul is to miss the whole point of life. I could say that with more certainty if I knew the whole point of life. To worry too much about Oscar Wilde and Andy Warhol is just a lot of vanity.

How should a person be? I sometimes wonder about it, and I can't help answering like this: a celebrity. But for all that I love celebrities, I would never move somewhere that celebrities actually exist. My hope is to live a simple life, in a simple place, where there's only one example of everything.

By *a simple life*, I mean a life of undying fame that I don't have to participate in. I don't want anything to change, except to be as famous as one can be, but without that changing anything. Everyone would know in their hearts that *I* am the most famous person alive—but not talk about it too much. And for no one to be too interested in taking my picture, for they'd all carry around in their heads an image of me that was unchanging, startling, and magnetic. No one has to know what I think, for I don't really think anything at all, and no one has to know the details of my life, for there are no good details to know. It is the quality of fame one is after here, without any of its qualities.

In an hour Margaux's going to come over and we're going to have our usual conversation. Before I was twenty-five, I never had any friends, but the friends I have now interest me nonstop. Margaux complements me in interesting ways. She paints my picture, and I record what she is saying. We do whatever we can to make the other one feel famous.

In this way, I should be satisfied with being famous to three or four of my friends. And yet it's an illusion. They like me for who I am, and I would rather be liked for who I *appear* to be, and for who I appear to be, to be who I am.

We are all specks of dirt, all on this earth at the same time. I look at all the people who are alive today and think, *These are my contemporaries. These are my fucking contemporaries!* We live in an age of some really great blow-job artists. Every era has its art form. The nineteenth century, I know, was tops for the novel.

I just do what I can not to gag too much. I know boyfriends get really excited when they can touch the soft flesh at the back of your throat. At these times, I just try to breathe through my nose and not throw up on their cock. I did vomit a little the other day, but I kept right on sucking.

Soon, the vomit was gone, and then my boyfriend pulled me up to kiss me.

Aside from blow jobs, though, I'm through with being the perfect girlfriend, just through with it. Then if he's sore with me, let him dump my ass. That will just give me more time to be a genius.

One good thing about being a woman is we haven't too many examples yet of what a genius looks like. It could be me. There is no ideal model for how my mind should be. For the men, it's pretty clear. That's the reason you see them trying to talk themselves up all the time. I laugh when they won't say what they mean so the academies will study them forever. I'm thinking of you, Mark Z., and you, Christian B. You just keep peddling your phony-baloney genius crap, while I'm up giving blow jobs in heaven.

My ancestors took what they had, which was nothing, and left their routines as slaves in Egypt to follow Moses into the desert in search of the promised land. For forty years they wandered through sand. At nights they rested where they could, against the dunes that had been built up by the winds. Waking the next morning, they took the flour from their sacks and moistened it with their spit and beat together a smooth dough, then set off, stooped, across the sand, the dough spread across their backs. It mingled with the salt of their sweat and hardened in the sun, and this is what they had for lunch. Some people spread the dough flat, and that dough became matzo. Others rolled tubes and fastened the ends, and those people ate bagels.

For so many years I have written *soul* like this: *sould*. I make no other consistent typo. A girl I met in France once said, *Cheer up! Maybe it doesn't actually mean you've sold your soul—* I was staring unhappily into my beer—*but rather that you never had a soul to sell.*

We were having Indian food. The man next to us was an Englishman, and he brightened up. He said, *It's so nice to hear English being spoken here! I haven't heard any English in weeks.* We tried not to smile, for smiling only encourages men to bore you and waste your time.

I thought about what that girl had said for a week. I was determined to start the task I had long been putting off, having for too long imagined it would take care of itself in the course of things, without my paying attention to it, all the while knowing in my heart that I was avoiding it, trying to patch myself together with my admiration for the traits I saw so clearly in everyone else. I said to myself sternly, *It's time to stop asking questions of other people. It is time to just go into a cocoon and spin your soul.* But when I got back to the city, I neglected this plan in favor of hanging out with my friends every night of the week, just as I had been doing before I'd left for the Continent.

The girl who had given me her condolences was in her midthirties, an American in Paris named Jen. She was a

friend of a friend and had, in a friendly way, accepted my
request to be put up for the nights I would be there. Her
job was doing focus groups for large corporations, including the United States Army, which wanted help with its
recruitment advertising. She had some ethical qualms about
this but was more concerned with her boyfriend, who had
suddenly started ignoring her. This was the central pre-
occupation of her life when I arrived, because it was the
more emotional.

There are certain people who do not feel like they were
raised by wolves, and they are the ones who make the world
tick. They are the ones who keep everything functioning so
the rest of us can worry about what sort of person we should
be. I have read all the books, and I know what they say:
You—but better in every way! And yet there are so many ways
of being better, and these ways can contradict each other!

   Yesterday Margaux told me a story that her mother often
tells about when she was a baby. It took Margaux a long
time to talk, and everyone thought she was a little dumb.
Margaux's mother had a friend who was a bit messed up and
really into self-help books and all sorts of self-improvement
tapes. One day, she had been telling Margaux's mother
about a technique in which, whatever problem you came
across in your life, you were just supposed to throw up your
hands and say, *Who cares?* That night, as Margaux's parents
and her slightly older sister were sitting around the dinner
table and Margaux was in her high chair, her sister spilled

her milk and the glass broke all across the table. Her mother started yelling, and her sister started crying. Then, from over in the high chair, they heard little Margaux going, *Who cares?*

I'm sorry, but I'm really glad she's my best friend. If I had known, when I was a baby, that in America there was a baby who was throwing up her hands and saying, first words out of her mouth, *Who cares?* and that one day she'd be my best friend, I would have relaxed for the next twenty-three years, not a single care in the world.

ACT

1

SHOLEM PAINTS

We were having brunch together. It was Sunday. I got there first, then Misha and Margaux arrived, then Sholem and his boyfriend, Jon.

A few weeks earlier, the owners had repainted the diner walls from a grease-splattered beige to a thicky pastel blue and had spray-painted giant pictures of scrambled eggs and strips of bacon and pancakes with syrup. It ruined the place somewhat, but the food was cheap, it was never crowded, and they always had a place for us.

I shared a breakfast special and a grilled cheese with Margaux. Jon asked for our fries. I don't remember what we started off talking about, or who was the funniest that day. I remember none of the details of our conversation until the subject turned to ugliness. I said that a few years ago I had looked around at my life and realized that all the ugly people had been weeded out. Sholem said he couldn't enjoy a friendship with someone he wasn't attracted to. Margaux said it was impossible for her to picture an ugly person, and Misha remarked that ugly people tend to stay at home.

These are a few of the sordid fruits that led to the Ugly Painting Competition.

When Sholem was a teenager, he had dreamed of being a theater actor, but his parents didn't want him to go to theater school. They didn't think it was practical, and encouraged him to go to art school instead. So he went, and his first year there, up late one night painting, as the sun began rising with the morning, a sudden and strong feeling came up inside him that said, *I must be an artist. I must paint for the rest of my life. I will not settle for anything else. No other future is acceptable to me.*

It was an epiphany and a decision both, from which there would be no turning back—the first and most serious vow of his life. So this past spring, he completed his M.F.A. thesis and graduated.

Who came up with the idea for the Ugly Painting Competition? I don't remember, but once I got enthusiastic, suddenly we all were. The idea was that Margaux and Sholem would compete to see who could make the uglier painting. I really hoped it would happen. I was curious to see what the results would be, and secretly I envied them. I wanted to be a painter suddenly. *I* wanted to make an ugly painting— pit mine against theirs and see whose would win. What would my painting look like? How would I proceed? I thought it would be a simple, interesting thing to do. I had spent so much time trying to make the play I was writing— and my life, and my self—into an object of beauty. It was exhausting and all that I knew.

Margaux agreed to the competition right away, but Sholem was reluctant. He didn't see the point. The premise turned him off so much—that one should *intentionally* make something ugly. *Why?* But I egged him on, pleading, and finally he gave in.

As soon as Sholem returned home after brunch, he set about making his entry—so he wouldn't have to think about it anymore, he explained to me later, or have looming before him the prospect of having to make something ugly.

He went straight into his studio, having already decided what he would do. He imagined it would be like this intellectual exercise that he could sort of approach in a cold fashion. He would just do everything he hated when his students did it. He started the composition smack-dab in the middle of a piece of paper, since paper is uglier than canvas. Then he painted a weird, cartoonish man in profile with fried-egg eyes, and he outlined things instead of shading them, delineating each individual eyelash. Instead of making a nostril, he sort of drew a hole. In the background he painted fluffy white clouds over orange triangular mountains. He made the background a gross pinkish-brownish gray, using mineral sediment dug up from the bottom of the jar in which he washed his brushes. For skin tone he just mixed red and white, and for the shadows he used blue. Though he thought in the end there would be some salvageable qualities to the painting, it just kept getting more and more disgusting until finally he began to feel so awful that he finished it off quickly. Dipping a thick brush in black paint, he wrote at the bottom, really carelessly, *The sun will come out tomorrow.* Then he stepped back and looked at the result, and found it so revolting that he had to get it out of his studio, and left it on the kitchen table to dry.

Sholem went out to get some groceries for dinner, but the entire time he was gone he felt nauseous. Returning home and setting the bags on the counter, he saw the painting lying there and thought, *I cannot see that thing every time I walk into the kitchen.* So he took it to the basement and left it near the washer and dryer.

From there, the day just got worse. Making the painting had set off a train of really depressing and terrible thoughts, so that by the time evening came, he was fully plunged in despair. Jon returned home, and Sholem started following him around the apartment, whining and complaining about everything. Even after Jon had gone into the bathroom and shut the door behind him, Sholem still stood on the other side, moaning about what a failure he was, saying that nothing good would ever happen to him, indeed that nothing good ever had; his life had been a waste. *It's like you work so hard to train a dog to be good!* he called through the door. *And*

the dog is your hand! Then one day you're forced to beat all the good-
ness out of that dog in order to make it cruel. That day was today!

Jon grunted.

Then Sholem plodded into the living room and sent an
email to the group of us, saying, *This project fills me with shame
and self-loathing. I just did my ugly painting, and I feel like I raped
myself. How's yours, Margaux?*

Margaux, the better artist, wrote back: *i spent all day on
my bed island reading the new york times.*

Fifteen years ago, there lived a painter in our town named Eli
Langer. When he was twenty-six, an artist-run center pre-
sented his first show. The paintings were gorgeous and
troubled, very masterful, all done in rich browns and reds.
They were moody and shadowy with old men, girls, and
plush chairs, windows, and naked laps. A sadness clouded
the few faces, which were obscured by darkness and lit only
by faint moonlight. The canvases were very large, and they
seemed like the work of someone with great assurance and
freedom.

After the show had been up for only a week, it was shut
down by the police. People claimed that the pictures were
child pornography. The canvases were confiscated, and they
were sentenced to be destroyed by the court.

The story was reported in newspapers all across the
country, and the trial played on TV for an entire year. Prom-
inent artists and intellectuals became involved and spoke

publicly and wrote editorials about artistic freedom. In the end, the judge ruled in Eli's favor, partly; the paintings were returned to him, but on the condition that no one ever see them again. He left them in a corner of his mother's attic, where they remain, covered in soot and mold, today.

After the trial was done, Eli felt exhausted and shaken. Now when he stepped before a canvas, brush in hand, he found that the spirit lay dead in him. He left Toronto for L.A., where he thought he might be able to feel more free, but the images still did not come as they had before.

Crushed with a new insecurity and inhibition, he applied to his now-tiny canvases only hesitant whites, or whites muddled with pink, or a bit of yellow, or the most apologetic blue—so that even if you stepped really close to the paintings, you could barely make out a thing. For the few solo shows he managed to complete in the years following the trial, he created only deeply abstract work, not anything even remotely figurative.

Several times a year, Eli would return to Toronto for a week or so, and would go to art parties and talk about painters and the importance of painting, and would speak confidently about brushstroke and color and line, and would do coke and be sensitive and brutish. On his forearms were tattooed twelve-point letters—the initials of local women artists he had loved, none of whom would speak to him anymore. The male painters embraced him like he was a prodigal son, and word always got around: *Have you seen Eli Langer? Eli's back in town!*

Late last winter, Margaux talked with him for the first time. They sat on an iron bench behind a gallery after an opening, surrounded by snow, warmed by a fire burning in a can.

Margaux worked harder at art and was more skeptical of its effects than any artist I knew. Though she was happier in her studio than anywhere else, I never heard her claim that painting mattered. She hoped it could be meaningful, but had her doubts, so worked doubly hard to make her choice of being a painter as meaningful as it could be. She never talked about galleries or went on about which brands of paint were best. Sometimes she felt bad and confused that she had not gone into politics—which seemed more straightforwardly useful, and which she thought she was probably well suited for, having something of the dictator inside, or something of the dictator's terrible certainty. Her first feeling every morning was shame about all the things wrong in the world that she wasn't trying to fix. And so it embarrassed her when people remarked on her distinctive brushstrokes, or when people called her work *beautiful*, a word she claimed not to understand.

Then that night, around a fire burning in a can, she and Eli spent several hours talking about color and brushstroke and line. They went on to email for several months, and she was briefly converted into the sort of painter he was— a painter who respected painting in itself. But after two months, her art crush dematerialized.

"He's just another man who wants to teach me something," she said.

. . .

Misha and I had planned to take a walk that afternoon, so I went to the apartment he and Margaux shared. When I arrived, he was in his study, at his computer, worrying over his life by checking his email.

We left together and walked north through the neighborhood. It was one of the few genuinely hot days we'd had that summer. As the sky went dark with dusk, I asked him whether Margaux had begun her ugly painting yet. He said he thought not. I said I was really eager to see the results.

Misha said, "It'll be really good for Sholem. He's so afraid of anything hippie."

"Is making an ugly painting hippie?" I asked him.

"It kind of is," he said. "There's, like, experimentation to no clearly valuable end. It's certainly more hippie than making a painting that you know is going to be good."

"Why should Sholem make a painting that he doesn't know is going to be good?"

"I don't know," he said. "But I do think Sholem has a fear of being bad, or of doing the wrong thing. He seems really afraid to take a wrong step at any moment, in any direction. And if what you're afraid of is to take a wrong step at any moment in any direction, that can be limiting. It's *good* for an artist to try things. It's *good* for an artist to be ridiculous. Sholem *should* be a hippie, because with him there's always a tremendous amount of caution."

"What's wrong with caution?"

"Well, there's a misunderstanding, isn't there? Isn't that

what was happening over brunch? Sholem was saying that freedom, for him, is having the technical facility to be able to execute whatever he wants, just whatever image he has in his mind. But that's not freedom! That's control, or power. Whereas I think Margaux understands freedom to be the freedom to take risks, the freedom to do something bad or to appear foolish. To not recognize that difference is a pretty big thing."

I said nothing, feeling tense. I wanted to defend Sholem, but I wasn't sure how.

"It's like with improv," Misha said. "True improv is about surprising yourself—but most people won't improvise truthfully. They're afraid. What they do is pull from their bag of tricks. They take what they already know how to do and apply it to the present situation. But that's cheating! And cheating's bad for an artist. It's bad in life—but it's really bad in art."

We had circled ten blocks and the sun had gone down as we were talking. The houses and trees were now painted a dark, dusky blue. Misha said he had a phone meeting, so we started back toward his apartment. His work life was strange and I didn't quite understand it, but neither did he, and it sometimes perplexed and saddened him. There seemed to be no structure or cohesion to it at all. He did only the things he was good at, and the things that gave him pleasure. Sometimes he taught improv classes to nonactors, sometimes he tried to keep nightclubs out of the Portuguese neighborhood where we lived, sometimes he hosted shows. There was no name you could give to it all. In the short biography he had submitted to Harvard—for what would become a dense, leather-bound volume for distribution at his fifteen-year college reunion—his classmates wrote lengthy entries about their worldly success, their children, and their spouses. Misha's entry had simply stated:

> Does anyone else feel really weird about having gone to Harvard, given the life they're living now? I live in a two-bedroom apartment above a bikini store in Toronto with my girlfriend, Margaux.

"Good night," I said.
"Good night."

Several years ago, when I was engaged to be married but afraid to go through with it—afraid that I would end up divorced like my parents, and not wanting to make a big mistake—I had gone to Misha with my concerns. We were drinking at a party and left to take a walk through the night, our feet brushing gently through the lightly fallen snow.

As we walked, I told Misha my fears. Then, after listening for a long while, he finally said, "The only thing I ever understood is that everyone should make the big mistakes."

So I took what he said to heart and got married. Three years later I was divorced.

chapter 2

AT THE POINT WHERE CONVICTION MEETS THE ROUGH TEXTURE OF LIFE

In the years leading up to my marriage, my first thought every morning was about wanting to marry.

One night, in a bar on a boat that was permanently docked at the harbor, I sat beside an old sailor. He had been watching me steadily as I drank. Then we started discussing children; he'd never had any, and I said I thought I would not, as I was certain my kid would be a bad kid. He said, bewildered, "How could anything not good come from *you*?"

I felt so moved then—shivering at the thought of a divine love that accepts us all, in our entirety. The bar around us became rich and saturated with color, as if all the molecules in the air were bursting their seams—each one insisting on its perfection too.

Then the moment was gone. I saw him as just an old

man staring at a girl—seeing her but seeing nothing. He didn't know my insides. There was something wrong inside me, something ugly, which I didn't want anyone to see, which would contaminate everything I would ever do. I knew the only way to repair this badness was devotion in love—the promise of my love to a man. Commitment looked so beautiful to me, like everything I wanted to be: consistent, wise, loving, and true. I wanted to be an ideal, and believed marrying would make me into the upright, good-inside person I hoped to show the world. Maybe it would correct my flightiness, confusion, and selfishness, which I despised, and which ever revealed my lack of unity inside.

So I thought about marriage day and night. And I went straight for it, like a cripple goes for a cane.

Several months before our wedding, my fiancé and I were strolling together in an elegant park when off in the distance we noticed a bride and a groom standing before a congregation, tall and upright like two figures on a cake. The audience was sitting on folding chairs in the afternoon sun, and we went over giddily to eavesdrop, crouching behind some false rocks, trying to be serious but giggling anyway. I could not see the groom's face—he was turned away—but the bride was facing me. The vows were being exchanged, and the minister was speaking quietly. Then I saw and heard the lovely bride grow choked up with emotion as she repeated the words *for richer or for poorer*. A tear ran down her cheek, and she had to stop and collect herself before she finished what she was saying.

As my fiancé and I walked away, I said that I thought it was a pretty vain, stupid, materialistic part to get choked up on—but we admitted that we did not know her financial history.

On the day of our wedding, my fiancé and I stood in a bay window before an audience of a dozen people—family and close friends—repeating our marriage vows as the secular minister spoke them.

Then something happened. As I said the words *for richer or for poorer*, that bride came up in me. Tears welled in my eyes, just as they had welled up in hers. My voice cracked with the same emotion that had cracked her voice, but I felt none of it. It was a copy, a possession, canned. That bride inhabited me at the exact moment I should have been most present. It was like I was not there at all—it was not me.

In the months and years of our marriage that followed, I recoiled, disgusted, whenever I recalled this scene—which was supposed to be among the most beautiful of my life. Some people look back on their wedding day as a reminder of their love, but I felt ever uncertain, thinking back upon it, about whether my marriage could truly be called *mine*.

I had lived with one man before my husband: my high school boyfriend—the first man I truly loved. We thought we would be together forever, or if we separated, that we would return to one another in the end.

Before we moved in together, we lived down the hall from each other on the second floor of a crummy rooming house in tiny, separate rooms. He sat at his desk and wrote plays, while I sat at my desk and wrote plays too. One evening, spying outside my door, he heard me talking on the phone with a friend about how I had a crush on a photographer in New York and thought it would be exciting to be with him. The photographer had invited me to live with him there as his girlfriend and assistant. He had taken some flattering pictures of me before leaving his home in Toronto, and I still thought about him a bit, sometimes.

My boyfriend, feeling hurt and jealous and betrayed, that night stole my computer from my room as I was sleeping and wrote on it till dawn, then returned it to my desk before I woke.

When I got up the next morning, I found, there on the screen, an outline for a play about my life—how it would unfold, decade by decade. Reading it compulsively as the sun came up in the window behind me, I grew incredibly scared. Tears rolled down my cheeks as I absorbed the terrible picture he had painted of my life: vivid and vile and filled with everything his heart and mind knew would hurt me best.

In the story, my desire to be with the photographer in New York started me on a path of chasing one fruitless prospect after the next, always dissatisfied, heading farther and farther away from the good, picking up men and dropping them. While my boyfriend rose in prestige and power, a loving family growing around him, I marched on toward my shriveled, horrible, perversion of an end, my everlasting seeking leaving me ever more loveless and alone. In the final scene I kneeled in a dumpster—a used-up whore, toothless, with a pussy as sour as sour milk—weakly giving a Nazi a blow job, the final bit of love I could squeeze from the world. I asked the Nazi, the last bubble of hope in my heart floating up, *Are you mine?* to which he replied, *Sure, baby*, then turned around and, using his hand, cruelly stuck my nose in his hairy ass and shat. The end.

I tried to forget his play, but I could not, and the more I pressed it away, the more it seared itself into my heart. It lodged inside me like a seed that I was already watching take root and grow into my life. The conviction in its every line haunted me. I was sure he could see my insides, as he was the first man who had loved me. I was determined to act in such a way as to erase the fate of the play, to bury far from my heart the rotting seed he had discovered—or planted—there.

What power a girl can have over a boy, to make him write such things! And what power a boy can have over a girl, to make her believe he has seen her fate. We don't know the effects we have on each other, but we have them.

Every other Wednesday during my marriage, our apartment was filled with smoke from the cigarettes of all our friends.

They drank in our rooms and made out on the fire escape. In the beginning, it felt like something truly important was happening. People came, and there was a bounty: cheese and grapes and bread and wine and all the alcohol you could drink.

But two years into our parties, I surveyed the scene from the corner and wondered, *Why are we having these parties?* What were we making, coming together like that? We were trying to prove that we had everything because we had parties, but I began to feel like we had nothing but parties. If anyone from the future could look back on what we were building, I was sure they would say, *That could only have been built by slaves.*

Friends passed through our doors. We laid out food and drinks. I started going to bed at one in the morning, then at midnight, then eleven, then ten. When finally everyone left at two or three or four, I would rise from bed and go downstairs, clean up the food, and cap the drinks. I would straighten the pillows, fix the chairs, sweep away the remnants of bread and cheese, dump out the cigarette butts and plastic cups. This was now my favorite part of the party.

When I was little, I was truly afraid that one day I would grow up and get divorced. As I got older, this fear grew with me, and upon getting engaged, the fear raised an anchor and threw it down in my very center. A fear can feel like a premonition, and so it was with me; before marrying, and once married, I never imagined the happy years that he and I might share. What I felt instead was dread—helpless before our marriage's inevitable end.

I felt like I was the tin man, the lion, and the scarecrow in one: I could not feel my heart, I had no courage, I could not use my brain.

One night at one of our parties, I went into the bathroom with my stomach rumbling. I sat on the toilet and waited for the massive shit that I knew was coming, while friends and strangers sat around the living room, or stood outside the door, talking and drinking. Sitting there, I recalled a dream from the night before, in which I was taking pills that made me shit a lot. In my dream, I decided I would only write what I thought about as I shit—since I was now spending all my time shitting. But I could not shit, sitting there at the party. I hated the thought that when I opened the door, I would reveal to everyone the shittiness that was mine. I stood up and buttoned my jeans, looked down into the empty bowl, and went to get a drink.

After pouring myself a gin and tonic, I noticed that my husband was talking close to someone I had never seen before, who was a sitting on the window ledge, talking loudly over him. She had bleached blond hair and dark, obvious roots. Her voice was deep. She had the pitless eyes of a cartoon character and a genuine nonchalance in her being, and she was dressed in a strange outfit: heavy boots, tall white socks over black leggings, and a pink corduroy jacket with white fluffy clouds. She looked at the same time like a little girl, a sexy woman, and a man.

My husband and I never observed much decorum about who we could talk or flirt with—half the whole point of the parties was to talk and flirt around a bit—but something about this scene was threatening. I didn't like his eagerness, how drunk he was getting, how alive and happy he seemed. It wasn't like watching him talk to other girls. I felt a jealousy spoil my blood, noticing the loose and confident way she had, her unmistakable freedom. *What does she have that I don't?* came into my head, like a thunderclap; a question that left me so ashamed that I turned away and made for the fire escape to smoke alone.

I was sitting on the iron steps in the coolish breeze, half finished with my cigarette, when the girl climbed out of the window and looked at me.

"Can I bum one?" she asked. "I lost my cigarettes in the street."

I handed over the pack, nervous inside. She told me her name was Margaux, and I told her my name was Sheila and lit her cigarette, then sat back, trembling inside. Had she come out here for *me*? An excitement rose in my being just to think it. But I didn't say a word. Instead, we smoked together quietly, and as she exhaled, the trees touched each other's branches in the wind.

Later, remembering that night, all I recalled was the physical distance between us. We began seeing each other all over the city. We would say hello, not much more. Then we started exchanging emails, making plans and breaking them. Somehow it felt okay. If I canceled, she was relieved; it gave her more time to paint. And whenever she canceled, I felt relieved, as I was eager to finish writing my play. Finally we made plans that neither of us got around to canceling in time. We would visit an art gallery a little north of the city.

We met up at the northernmost subway station and waited for the bus. When we got on, we learned from the driver that it would be a forty-minute drive—something neither of us had anticipated.

And the whole way up, and the whole way back, we sat there silently, too intimidated by the other to say a thing.

chapter 3

SHEILA AND MARGAUX

One month later, I received an invitation to Margaux's birthday party. I considered going, but in the end, I did not. I had more pressing things to do—like work on my play and make it perfect. I also figured her party would be filled with all sorts of interesting and impressive people who were closer to her than I was; that she would just glance at me from the corner and wave.

My husband left our house for hers, and I was fast asleep when he came home.

One week later, Sheila receives an email from Margaux . . .

1. i have always admired a lack of social obligation. in fact, i aspire to it. the number of birthday parties i

attend is too many. apart from that, i assumed you weren't coming to my party and you did not.

2. at my party, your husband, probably being nothing but sweet and drunk and feeling generous, and probably having nothing to do with your sentiments, said, "hell, you and sheila should spend more time together."

3. and i laughed and thought nothing of it.

4. but then when i saw you on the street yesterday, i was very annoyed and probably annoying. my annoyance was unfair and a little silly.

5. i could never find fault in someone for choosing not to be my friend. but i was disappointed not to have a girl, after searching high and low.

6. but the boys i know might be girly enough for me. and girly boys are much easier to boss around than a girl, of course.

7. to sum up, i'm not very smooth with married women, am i? but i will relax a little.

8. no response required, my pet, especially if i have hurt or troubled you.

I was thrown off by this email—I had not figured that my presence at her party would mean a single thing! I went to take a walk to sort out how I felt and how I ought to reply. As I wandered through the neighborhood, I zipped and unzipped my jacket as my body went from hot to cold.

Strolling beneath the sun, I realized I'd never had a woman either. I supposed I didn't trust them. What was a

woman for? Two women was an alchemy I did not understand. I hadn't been close to a girl since Angela broke my
heart when I was ten years old and told all of my secrets to
everyone. It would have been so easy to count the ways I
had been betrayed by girls, all the ways I had been hurt by
them. And if I wanted, I could have as easily made a list of
all the girls to whom I had caused pain. First there was
Lorraine.

But it was not that way with men. Ever since I was a
teenager, I had been drawn to men exclusively, and they
drew themselves to me—as lovers, as friends. *They* pursued
me. It was simple. It was men I enjoyed talking to at parties,
and whose opinions I was interested in hearing. It was men
I wanted to grow close to and be influenced by. It was easy.
There was a way in which I felt they would always come
home. The good ones had a natural regard for me, and
there was always an attempt to treat me nicely. Even if they
could be neglectful or forgetful, they were rarely cruel, and
though they weren't necessarily so reliable, they were trust-
worthy in the deeper sense: I never worried that a man's
heart would turn against me—at least not before mine
turned against him—and certainly not for no reason at all.
There would always be a veil over their eyes when they
looked at me, which was a kind of protection.

With a woman, who was too much the same, it never
felt that way. So much had to be earned—but no earnings
built up! Trust had to be won from zero at every encounter.
That's the reason you always see women being so effusive
with each other—crying out shrilly upon recognizing each

other in the street. Women always have to confirm with each other, even after so many years: *We are still all right.* But in the exaggeration of their effusiveness, you know that things are *not* all right between them, and that they never will be. A woman can't find rest or take up home in the heart of another woman—not permanently. It's just not a safe place to land. I knew the heart of a woman could be a landing ground for a man, but for a woman to try to land in another woman's heart? That would be like landing on something wobbly, without form, like trying to stand tall in Jell-O. Why would I want to stand tall in Jell-O?

Yet there were things in Margaux's email I could not resist. I admired her courage, her heart, and her brain. I envied the freedom I suspected in her, and wanted to know it better, and become that same way too.

Back at home, I emailed her to say that I regretted missing her party, explaining that I'd thought I would finish my play that night. I said I would drop by her studio with champagne soon to make it up.

Then I went to bed. My husband was out drinking somewhere.

My first day of typing school, I sat there resolute. The instructor stood before us like a piece on a chessboard. She was stiff and without divinity. I knew I would learn nothing from such a wooden shoe.

I sat up straight and smiled at everyone in their seats. I wanted all those liars on my side. I wanted them to stand up and cheer my name later in the semester—to be a hero to all those liars! It didn't even matter that they were liars. I was willing to be a hero even to liars. Even to thieves! I hoped my smiling would convince them all of my good-naturedness. At the very root of me, I hoped they would see, was a friendly idiot who didn't know her own interests. With this in their minds, they'd relate to me as a peer, I hoped, and would one day let me lead them.

I prayed I wouldn't create any enemies, as I had done in football school. There, all of my plans backfired. The jocks seemed to have more integrity of spirit than I did. They weren't going to let some withered wanderer with half a plan lead them. By the end of the first afternoon, they were laughing at me. The next morning, I went in wearing a different sweater, but they still knew it was me and stuffed me in a locker. I saw I wasn't going to outwit them. Those people didn't deal in wit. Even if I *did* outwit them, that wouldn't shake them. Their assurance was rooted in something deeper, more solid, from which it flowed.

I should have stuck around to discover the nature of that soil for myself—but I belong with the liars and weaklings. I cannot lead my betters. If I want to be a hero, it will not be to the jocks, whose interiors have an integrity that springs up from the very center of the earth itself. It will be to the utter liars I find myself sitting with here, in the white-walled room that is the typing school's second-floor studio.

Photocopied and handed out to us at the beginning of class was a second-rate artist's rendering of the placement of the keys as you would find them on a real typewriter.

"Hold on to it," we were told. "This will be your type-writer for the next two weeks."

One morning, Sheila finds an email from Margaux . . .

1. i'm free:
2. this afternoon, night
3. tomorrow afternoon, night
4. the next afternoon, night and day
5. just hiding inside painting
6. wearing a matching tracksuit and listening to the bbc.

They continue to write back and forth. Margaux emails Sheila . . .

1. there was a robbery and they're blaming it on me.
2. i can't leave the neighborhood! i haven't felt this at home in decades!
3. legally i don't think they can make me leave but they live above me and work below me and my tolerance is gone.
4. i was pretty upset, but now i'm glad. i have decided to find a much better studio with an absentee landlord.
5. i'm scouring the neighborhood with my cell phone.

1. selena's gallery is having a private viewing of an artist whose one previous show i saw. it's a fancy exclusive affair with lots of directors, curators, and free martinis or something.

2. you and i have very personally not been invited.
3. i heard gossip that selena felt pretty stupid about telling me she didn't like female writers. i nodded.

1. i've been throwing out old art for the last couple of days, trying hard not to, trying hard to, but i just now figured that it's only fair to explain to you who i am, so i am emailing you my very first painting (17 yrs of age—i wish i could say 14 but the date is written on it along with my very fancy signature) even though i want to throw it out.
2. and i found my cigarettes in the street!
3. my paintings look pretty good when i'm wearing your special glasses. thank you.

1. misha and i were taking a walk this afternoon. we passed a *please come in for our open house* sign. we went through a small little door in a fence into a small little garden into a small little house. it was leaning about 5 degrees to the left. the windows open like doors and the bedroom is the size of a car.
2. i thought maybe you could buy it. "it's 240 thousand, no money down," the meek woman said, "and 100 years old."
3. i wish i could buy a house for a friend like i can buy a cake.
4. if you're curious about what i think you look like as a house, you should see it.

1. i am surprised at how much i miss you, like a real teenage girl.

1. hello. i was wondering, if you have red bike lights, could i borrow them tomorrow night?

1. i'm going to paint your portrait a hundred times and never mention it to anyone—articulately.

1. yes, i would like to see you. i have all the time in the world.

When I was little, I would lie in bed and stare at the ceiling in the darkened room at night, and quietly sing the song we had been taught in Hebrew school on the first day of the year, which we sang every morning.

Love is something if you give it away,
Give it away, give it away,
Love is something if you give it away,
You end up having more.

Love is like a magic penny!
Hold on tight and you won't have any!
Lend it, spend it, you'll have so many,
They'll roll all over the floor, oh!

This seemed impossible to me, just crazy! If you give it away you'll end up having *more*? It was the only poem I knew and my favorite one, for it baffled me. I recited it over and over to myself, as if there was something I could learn from it. In my head, in rooms in homes, zillions of pennies rolled all over the floors, thick and encompassing like waves.

While I was lying there, overcome with wonder like that, Margaux was down in Texas, fighting with the popular girls beneath the harsh Texas sun. The afternoon of her grade-six graduation ceremony, she knew she would have to climb the stairs of the gym and stand on stage before everyone to receive an award for being the smartest kid in the school. That morning, as she was getting dressed, she went into her father's closet and pulled out a brown suit and her father's brown shoes and stuffed them in a duffel bag and took them with her as she left the house. Right before the announcement, she put them on and walked across the stage, the arms of his jacket hanging low beneath her hands, the cuffs of his pants bunched and dragging, to the laughter of the audience, her dignity intact.

For so long I had been looking hard into every person I met, hoping I might discover in them all the thoughts and feelings I hoped life would give me, but hadn't. There are some people who say you have to find such things in yourself, that you cannot count on anyone to supply even the smallest crumb that your life lacks.

Although I knew this might be true, it didn't prevent me from looking anyway. Who cares what people say? What people say has no effect on your heart.

chapter 4

SHEILA CAN'T FINISH HER PLAY

Margaux wanted to take me for ice cream in the park.

I was living in a crummy basement apartment, having just left my marriage and the suffocating feeling of leading a life that was not my own. I couldn't understand how it had come to that. I briefly considered leaving Toronto for L.A., but I had a fear that with my soul gone missing, if I left the place we had last been in together, it might not know where to find me if it wanted to return. What if it came looking for me and I was gone? So I stayed, but ever since moving out, my days had been upside down and strange. I could not tell what season it was, or if I was moving through water or air.

I heard a kick at the window—the doorbell didn't work—and I peeked out and saw Margaux's legs. I was so happy to see her. Every time it was a pleasure, and it really felt like we were coming to some new meaning. I called for her to wait and quickly finished dressing.

The night before, I had made out with a man in a bar. On his hands were warts—big ones covering his palms and wrists—and I let him put his acrid saliva all up and down my face and neck. It had given me satisfaction that he was so ugly. This is the great privilege of being a woman—we get to decide. I have always welcomed the hunchbacks with a readiness I can only call justice.

As we walked to the park, I asked Margaux if she had begun her ugly painting yet.

"Not yet," she said.

When we arrived at the park, we discovered the ice cream truck was gone, so we lay on our backs with our heads in the grass and watched the tree branches float above us. We talked for a while about this and that, then Margaux asked me how my play was going.

If I had known she was going to ask me that, I would never have gone to the park.

I had spent the past few years putting off what I knew I had to do—leave the world for my room and emerge with the moon, something upon which the reflected light of my experience and knowledge could be seen: a true work of art, a real play. I had been avoiding the theater's calls and felt ashamed—my distress only growing as the time I spent on the play expanded, as the good work I had done represented an ever smaller percentage of the time I had applied to it. A feminist theater company had commissioned me to write it during my first year of marriage, and my only question had been, "Does it have to be a feminist play?"

"No," they said, "but it has to be about women."

I didn't know anything about women! And yet I hoped I could write it, being a woman myself. I had never taken a commission before, but I needed the money, and figured I could just as easily lead the people out of bondage with words that came from a commissioned play as I could writing a play that originated with me. So I accepted, but the whole time I was married, I was concerned only with men—my husband in particular. What women had to say to one another, or how a woman might affect another, I did not know. I put off giving them the play and put it off until I hoped the theater would forget and stop calling me, but they did not.

Now that I had left my marriage and had moved into an apartment of my own, my mind was free to think of anything I wanted, and I vowed to return to the play with new vigor, but it had not yet happened. No amount of work could compensate for what I had lost since my decision to marry—a feeling of ease, of having some direction in the world. And I had once felt the benevolent operation of destiny in every moment! For most of my life, one thing led to the next. Each step bore its expected fruit. Every coincidence felt preordained. It was like innocence, like floating in syrup. People were brought to me. Luck unfurled at the slightest touch. I had a sense of the inevitability of things

as they occurred. Every move felt part of a pattern, more
intelligent than I was, and I merely had to step into the
designated place. I knew this was my greatest duty—this
was me fulfilling my role.

But once I was married, my relationship to my destiny
began to change. The signs grew more obscure. It was not
enough to read them once. I had to consult them again and
again to try and figure out the best direction, which would
lead me down a path to an end I could admire.

I was always second-guessing myself, always changing
my mind. I would return down the wrong road, then set
off along what I hoped was the right one. Destiny became
like an opaque, demanding, poorly communicative parent,
and I was its child, ever trying to please it, to figure out
what it wanted from me. I tried to read its face for clues to
understand how it wanted me to behave. In all of this, there
was an overarching question that never left my mind, an
ongoing task that could never be called complete, though I
hoped one day it would be: What was the right way to react
to people? Who was I to talk to at parties? How was I to *be*?

But in answer to this, the universe gave me no solid signs.
That didn't prevent me from looking, anyway, or from believing an answer was out there. It was, in a sense, how I spent
all my time, for how else could I make the universe love me?
If I did things badly, I would surely lose all its favors, all its
protection—as if the universe would delight in me for being
a certain way.

Living in that house with my husband, I could not escape my every mistake; the walls were permanently scuffed with all the dark marks I had made while foolishly living. All I saw were the smudges, prominently there on what otherwise would have been a pure white wall.

Since the beginning, there had been an empathy between me and my husband; there had always been a sweetness. It was like we were afraid of breaking the other. We never fought or pushed, as though the world was hard enough. As for difficult conversations that might hurt the other—we left those matters alone. It could have gone on—our life and our love—but a few years into my marriage, I tripped. I tripped and stumbled and I regained my step, but in the wrong place this time, and my days began to mirror exactly, in smell and sensation, a monthlong period when I was eighteen: a hot and sticky August. I'd just moved out of the house I had been living in with my high school boyfriend, and was now in my father's basement. It was a month of limbo, between life in a house with my boyfriend and the freedom of theater school in another town.

That month, I experienced a tense idleness waiting for my new life to begin. It was a month of impatience, of stillness, like being set in amber. A certain smell followed me everywhere, like the smell of rotten candy. My insides were queasy. My skin was always sweating.

A vivid echo of those days, a living memory of it, entered my life again, came into my marriage, and remained with me for a whole six months. I wanted to break out of that loop—it felt terrible; something a person should not experience—just wrong! Every day should feel new, but I was back in the atmosphere of another time; one I had lived in already.

Every morning I woke up beside my husband and looked around to see if the feeling was still there; it always was. And I would get up for the day, exhausted by it already, sticky with the same tense idleness I had felt back then.

Then one day, without warning, the air pressure dropped. The feeling was just gone. I had done nothing to make it go. I looked about me, relieved. But it was only a pause, for then began a building-up, a feeling worse than what had come before, like I was about to hurtle through space and time, like I was a rock that had been placed into a slingshot, drawn back to that August and held there. Then the hand let me go.

I felt the blood inside me gathering fast, the pulse drum up in my ears, my skin grow tense and cold, like I was pushing through the atmosphere too fast. My body was filled to bursting with dread, the anticipation of something I did not know, and an equal resistance overtook me—I wanted nothing more than to stave off this terrifying end to which I was hurtling, which I saw in my head as some kind of pain, and which was accompanied by a phrase that went through my head, over and over again: *Punch yourself through a brick wall, punch yourself through a brick wall.*

One evening, I saw what the brick wall was: my marriage. A tension came over me, an unbearable feeling of just wanting to get it over with. The wall was there; the pressure could only be released one way. I sat on my hands the entire day, but inside I was hurtling through space and time like a rock, and I told myself not to see anyone—not to speak to anyone—but when my husband lay down beside me that night, I turned over and said, as though I had thought it all through, considered his side, and was making a thoughtful decision: "I cannot be with you anymore."

He'd had no sense of the storm clouds that had been building within me, and when he slammed out of the room, the storm clouds burst into rain, and all over my face and body was the cool wet of relief.

The next morning, I woke up in our bed alone. It was almost noon. I turned my head to look out the window. The sun was shining. I sat up and smelled the air, and I could tell I was in a new day. Those six months were over. The hurtling feeling was gone. That time was permanently behind me now, and I knew it would never visit me again. I felt an unbelievable joy; a freedom such as I could not remember feeling since I was a child. There was a lightness all through me, and I told myself, *This is the happiest day of your life.*

I slept on and off all day, exhausted, like someone who has been washed ashore on an island, safe and still and dry. The whipping about in the waves that had propelled me into my husband's arms, through our marriage, then suddenly away from him, had died down; the sea was calm and rolled back. I stood up on the sand and looked about me. I was alone, and I was free.

I knew that from then on I would have to make decisions without any footprints in the sand to follow, without any hand guiding my path. There would be no telling what would lead to what. I would have to use my judgment—not just my intuition. I would have to weigh things, take responsibility. I would have to look out at reality, not only within myself.

I was finally in the midst of the universe's indifference. It was like my mom and pop had died. It was up to me to choose. I saw that I could try and return to my husband if I wanted, but that this would not be destined, but my choice, but that this was no more required of me than not returning to my husband, which would also be a choice. The difference in these two paths had no intrinsic value—just difference. I could finally make up my own mind. I would have to decide how to be.

Living alone in my new apartment, I spent months staring at the play I had written under the influence of destiny. The first draft had come to me in that other time, and though not great, it seemed like it had been written by someone who had been living in some other world entirely. Finishing it now felt like an impossibility. Any direction I might take with it seemed as likely as any other. I didn't know what mark on earth I should make.

Of course, I did not know how to say any of this, or how to tell anyone any of this. I also didn't know why I would tell it, or what telling it might mean, or who I could tell it to—not Margaux, not Misha, not anyone I knew—none of whom had time for words like *destiny*.

So I turned to Margaux and said what I always said whenever anyone asked how the play was going. "Fine."

Then I stood up from the grass, brushed myself off, and said I had to go to the salon.

ACT

2

chapter 1

SHEILA GOES TO THE SALON

Since leaving my marriage, I had been working at a beauty salon.

When I was in high school, I had done a career test to see what career I was most suited for. There were three hundred questions: Would you rather mow the lawn or rock a baby? Would you rather groom a horse or make dinner? Would you rather shit in the toilet or on the floor? When I went to the guidance counselor for the results, she handed me some stapled forms that listed six hundred careers. Beside each career was a line, and along each line was a star. The farther to the right of the page the star was, the more suited to that career you were.

Most careers I was not cut out for. With others, like photographer, the star went halfway across. But one star went all the way to the farthest right margin of the page and almost off it: *hairdresser.* Of all the people in the world, hair-dressers were the people most like me. And so I always had it in the back of my head that this was the job I was most suited for and which would give me the most pleasure. When I compared it with finishing my play, it seemed so nice and easy.

I brought this up with my Jungian analyst, worried about money and frustrated at wasting my time with a play that was going nowhere. She said I should speak to a hair-dresser she had seen for many years—a German man named Uri who ran a salon a bike ride from where I lived. He was a very cultured man, she told me, and he liked mentoring young people. I held on to his number for a few months, then lost it, then found it and wrote him a letter, explaining that I had long dreamed of being a hairdresser, and could I meet him to talk about working there?

The salon was in a high-end commercial building with a large bookstore, a ritzy shoe store, a perfume shop, and two expensive restaurants. The salon was very spacious, with a pink-and-white color scheme. Many stylists were at work at their stations on the day that I arrived. Uri came out from his office to meet me. He was a tall and impressive man with lots of white hair and a youthful air, strength and vital-ity, good posture, and an elegant and engaging manner. His wife, Ruby, who was waiting for us in the office, was dressed all in white and was very feminine with light hair, lovely curves, and an appealing, girlish quality.

The three of us spoke for fifteen minutes. Uri cautioned me that many people had fantasies of becoming a hair-

dresser, but that it was a lot of work and not a game. I
assured him that there was no one more suited to this job
than me, and, nodding his head, he offered me some shifts.
"Do you want them?" he asked, and I said, "I do," welling
up with meaning, gratitude, and responsibility, like a real
bride.

Misha and Margaux seemed happy for me. They could tell
how much I enjoyed being at the salon. I felt suited to it
too. I dressed up nicely every day and made sure to move
elegantly while I was there, wanting to express in every
pore of my being the beauty that people came to a salon to
experience. When my birthday arrived, Misha gave me a
book called *Hair Heroes*, which profiled the most important
hairdressers of the twentieth century. In it, one of the hair-
dressers is quoted as saying, "I know all the secrets of the
Western world—but I'll never tell!"

The secrets of the Western world! I had found my kin.

My tasks were varied but limited. I shampooed the clients
and cleaned up—collected dirty towels from the bins by the
basins, put them in the wash, then put them in the dryer and
folded them perfectly and returned them to the shelves by
the bins. It was work I could believe in; making people look
and feel their best. I swept up hair and washed the plastic
bowls used to mix and apply the color. I moved about the
floor as if on a stage, fluidly and with ease. There was a great

simplicity to my life when I was there, and I looked forward to going, and I was never bored. I knew what was expected of me, and I was happy that I could comply. It fulfilled my serving instincts—my desire to uplift humanity. I knew nothing bad could happen in a hair salon, and nothing out of the ordinary ever did. I felt more comfortable and safe there than I had ever felt anywhere. The days I spent at home, working on my play, were miserable days; I longed to be at the salon. When I was at the salon, I wished to be nowhere else.

One day, watching me wipe down the basins, Uri came up beside me, put his heavy hand on my shoulder, and said, "I have decided to teach you everything I know." I bowed my head in gratitude.

Uri had been a stylist since he was fifteen years old. His mother had owned a salon, and she had supported herself during the war by cutting hair. He learned from this that a hairstylist could go anywhere in the world, live in any conditions, and always be able to feed his family. All he needed was his talent and the scissors in his hand.

One afternoon he wanted to show me a cut, and I stood near and observed as he chopped away at the woman's puffy brown hair in the back. "Most people would rather have more hair," he said, "but if the hair at the sides is thinner than at the back, you have to cut away some of the hair at the back in order that the head be balanced. Balance masks flaws," he told me. I wanted to write this on my arm.

SHEILA

I need some help with the play, and I thought that maybe by talking it over with you—I thought maybe you could help me figure out why it isn't working. Then I can listen to what we say, and think it over at home, and figure out where I'm going wrong.

Margaux shakes her head.

MARGAUX

First, I haven't read your play. Secondly, I don't have any answers.

SHEILA

It's okay that you haven't read the play. I think the problem is with what happens, so I'll just tell you the plot.

MARGAUX

Why are you looking to me for answers? I don't know anything you don't know!

SHEILA

I'm not looking to you for answers! Why would you say that? I was just hoping that if I—

MARGAUX

Don't you know that what I fear most is my words floating separate from my body? You there with that tape recorder is the scariest thing!

SHEILA

But the answer might be in something *I* say! Besides, who's
going to hear it?

MARGAUX

I don't know! I don't know where things end up! Then
whatever I happen to say, someone will believe I really said it
and meant it? No. No. You there with that tape recorder just
looks like my own death.

Sheila sighs deeply and looks out the window. Margaux looks out
the window, too. They do not talk for several minutes. Sheila
brushes some sand from the tabletop onto the floor.

As Margaux and I sat there, I tried to be compassionate. I
thought about how difficult it is to live in this world without any clothes on. I know it's the gods who determine
who among us is fated to go through life with her clothes
off. When the gods gather around a baby in its cradle and
dole out their gifts and curses, this is one aspect of things
they consider.

Most people live their entire lives with their clothes on,
and even if they wanted to, couldn't take them off. Then
there are those who cannot put them on. They are the ones
who live their lives not just as people but as examples of
people. They are destined to expose every part of themselves,
so the rest of us can know what it means to be a human.

Most people lead their private lives. They have been given a natural modesty that feels to them like morality, but it's not—it's luck. They shake their heads at the people with their clothes off rather than learning about human life from their example, but they are wrong to act so superior. Some of us have to be naked, so the rest can be exempted by fate.

MARGAUX

(*sighs*) All right. You know I have more respect for your art than I do for my own fears.

SHEILA

Thank you! Thank you!

MARGAUX

Just promise you won't betray me.

SHEILA

(*reassuringly*) I don't even know what that means.

Sheila beckons to the waitress, who comes over.

Can we also get some jam?

The waitress nods and leaves.

Is it too much that I asked for jam *and* water?

MARGAUX

(*suspiciously*) No.

Sheila clears her throat.

SHEILA

Okay. So what happens in the play is this: There are these two families, the Oddis and the Sings. And they each have a twelve-year-old kid. The Oddis have a twelve-year-old girl named Jenny, and the Sings have a twelve-year-old boy named Daniel. So both families are vacationing in Paris, and in the first scene of the play, the two families meet at a parade—

MARGAUX

Wait! Were they always meeting in Paris?

SHEILA

By accident. It's an accident. So they meet in Paris by accident because the kids recognize each other at a parade, and there's this sort of inexplicable hostility between the two mothers. They hate each other instantly, right?

MARGAUX

Right.

SHEILA

And at the end of the first scene, Daniel goes missing, 'kay?

MARGAUX

Okay.

Margaux takes some potatoes with a fork. They fall. She eats them with her fingers.

SHEILA

Then the next scene's back at the hotel. Now the problem of the play is: The kid's gone missing. But nobody reacts in a conventional way to it. Jenny really wants to find Daniel, but she becomes a more minor character in the play, and the real central character of the play becomes Ms. Oddi, Jenny's mother, who sort of realizes through the course of things, really quickly, that she's completely dissatisfied in her life and has never reached her full potential, blah blah blah. In the first draft of the play she runs away to the beach—to Cannes.

MARGAUX

Wait! Why does she run away?

SHEILA

She feels she's kind of been oppressed by her family.

MARGAUX

I guess she has no feelings for them. Or how else could she run away?

SHEILA

Huh? I guess she's distracting herself. Oh, and then she has this affair with the Man in the Bear Suit. At the end of the play, Daniel comes home, and it turns out he actually *ran* away. He has grown up in this really weird way, and he speaks this weird monologue about how great it is to be a grown-up. Anyways, now Ms. Oddi doesn't go to Cannes.

MARGAUX

(*disappointed*) Oh, she doesn't?

SHEILA

No. 'Cause the director, Ben, thought it would be better to localize the action at the hotel—

MARGAUX

Oh, I guess that *is* how theater works.

SHEILA

Yeah. So *now* what sets Ms. Oddi off is that they're in the hotel room and she's playing the flute, and Jenny never knew that she played the flute, and somebody from the hotel comes and asks if she'll play for dinner tonight—

MARGAUX

Yeah?

SHEILA

And . . . she doesn't.

MARGAUX

(*disappointed*) Oh.

SHEILA

'Cause she realizes she hasn't been playing all these years. She loved it but never took it seriously, and now she's afraid she's not good enough.

MARGAUX

Wait. Where did the flute come from?

SHEILA

The suitcase.

Margaux laughs.

So *now* we've got Ms. Oddi, who somehow—she feels she has to change her life—but she just keeps getting embroiled with all these various men from the hotel when all she wants to do is play her flute!

MARGAUX

The flute's my favorite part.

SHEILA

It's stupid!

MARGAUX

(*laughing*) It's just an autobiography.

Sheila puts her head in her hands.

SHEILA

I know, I *know*! But my life keeps changing. My life keeps changing!

MARGAUX

Well, it's too bad she never plays the flute. It's like when in films there's a painting that's being discussed, but you never— and all you want is to see this painting—but you never get to see it. It always seems nice to never see the painting because then it becomes so much more amazing than you could ever imagine!

SHEILA

(*unhappy*) Yeah.

Margaux picks up a thing of jam.

MARGAUX

Did you take one of these already?

SHEILA

Yes.

Margaux puts the jam on her plate.

In fact, I should pull the play.

MARGAUX

Pull the play?

SHEILA

(*miserable*) Too late now. Oh my God, Margaux, what am I going to *do*? The play's never made any sense! It's nonsense!

MARGAUX

How is that possible? You've been working on it for *years*!

SHEILA

I should have totally fucking never agreed to write this play in the first place! Oh my God. Maybe I can go into our studio and just spend all day . . .

MARGAUX

I mean, I guess you *could* spend all day . . .

SHEILA

But I can't fix the play in one day! If I can't fix it in three years, I can't fix it in a day! I have a real psychological block! I haven't been able to bring myself to finish it or work on it—I don't know why!

MARGAUX

Oh, it's so scary. Maybe you could come up with an alternative to the play. Maybe you could think of an alternative—

SHEILA

(*panicked*) An alternative *what*? An alternative way of writing it, or an alternative for what they could do?

MARGAUX

Maybe something about it being theater is really, like, blocking you. Maybe you could say, "What I've written is not interesting—here is something else you could do. If you don't want to do that, I'm sorry, but maybe you should pick someone else."

SHEILA

But they don't *want* to pick someone else! And they want a production! They want a *play*. There are so many *interesting* things one could do with a theater in three weeks. That I would *love* to do! That would be really interesting!

MARGAUX

Yeah, they want a play. Man, are they missing out. I really feel like theater hasn't caught up from a 1930s awareness. Do you want some of my toast? 'Cause this is a lot of toast.

SHEILA

Oh my God. Why are we *doing* this? I should have totally fucking said no last September!

MARGAUX

So what? They want to start getting actors and stuff?

SHEILA

They want to have a workshop in February and a main stage production in the spring. I should pull the play. There has never been a draft that anyone's been happy with. Not me, not the producer, not the director, not the other director we had.

Margaux eats the toast with jam.

MARGAUX

It still seems like you might do something in the next day that's remarkable. Maybe that's what the play could be about.

SHEILA

(*anxiously*) What? Saving the day?

MARGAUX

Something remarkable.

SHEILA

(*uncertain*) Yeah.

Long pause. Margaux is staring out the window.

What? What are you thinking?

MARGAUX

Sorry, sorry, I'm just trying to think of—of things I've given up on.

Pause.

No. I can't think of anything.

chapter 4

SHEILA WANTS TO LIVE

Twenty minutes later, Sheila and Margaux walk down the street to the Katharine Mulherin Gallery, where they recently began sharing a small studio on the second floor. Margaux unlocks the glass door, and they walk past the hung paintings to a rickety stairwell at the back. Sheila has been thinking about the crazy impressiveness of Margaux never having quit anything. She follows Margaux up the back steps.

SHEILA

But *listen*, Margaux! Otto Rank says that one day there will be no art, only artists—so the work of art is *renounced*! And I agree! I'm renouncing this play because it's not in service of my life. But if the primary thing was the work, I'd spend all of my time on the play. But you know what? This does not serve my life!

MARGAUX

Right.

SHEILA

Don't you think that's what's going on?

MARGAUX

No.

SHEILA

No, no! In Otto Rank's construction of it!

MARGAUX

We-ll . . .

They walk across an old rug into their dirty, white-walled studio.

I *do* think it's responsible not to put out a crappy play—in an old-fashioned, like, a strict old-fashioned sense. You shouldn't put out bad work. But if it's not about the work, then it doesn't matter how crappy it is. What matters is the people you're doing it with, and the experience you have doing it. Actually, I think it would be *way* more in service of your life to put out this mediocre play, so you could—

SHEILA

(*with angst*) *More* in service of my life! But my life suffers if I make bad—if I put out a bad play!

MARGAUX

That's right. So . . . Otto would say, *Who cares?*

Margaux starts setting things up on her drafting board.

SHEILA

No, no! Otto would say I'm doing the right thing! 'Cause if I want my life to be a work of art, then if I make bad work, it tarnishes my life. All I'm trying to say is that what you said earlier I think is *true*. We make art insofar as it enhances our life, and insofar as it adds to the beauty of life—

MARGAUX

Right.

SHEILA

—'cause as you say, it feels good to work hard—

MARGAUX

Yeah.

SHEILA

—it feels good to create something beautiful—

MARGAUX

Yeah.

SHEILA

—but not beyond that to the point where life suffers!

MARGAUX

So . . . you would have had to work really hard for this—
right—for this play that might not have served you.

SHEILA

(*sighs*) I don't know about the play. I don't know.

· chapter 5 ·

ISRAEL

That night, after spending several hours staring at my miserable play, I shut down my computer in frustration and left my apartment. I went to a party to celebrate the appearance of three more books of poetry in the world.

The party was in a wide and cavernous room with a large stage up front and the ceiling painted brown, draped around the sides with brown velvet. A large disco ball rotated in the center, and everything was polished wood and semiformal and awful.

Standing alone at the bar, I wondered if I could love the boy I noticed at the end of it—the one with the curly brown hair, who was like a washed-out, more neutral version of the first boy I loved. When he stepped out onto the front steps, I thought, *If he has gone out there to smoke, I will love him.* But when I got outside, though I could see a cigarette dangling from his lips, I did not love him.

I went back inside to get another drink and was standing by the bar when a man, slightly taller than me, stepped out from the crowd and moved toward me. My stomach lurched. I turned away. I was so attracted, I couldn't let myself speak. I knew him, though; his name was Israel. This was a guy whose girlfriend I had complimented the year before, running into her on the street and saying, "Your boyfriend is the sexiest guy in the city." Though I meant it, I was also hoping to flatter her. Later, when I learned that she was angry at me for saying this, I got upset. I had genuinely wanted to compliment her.

I had met Israel once before, several years ago, and I never forgot it. I was married at the time and was going down in an elevator in a building of artists' studios. He entered on the same floor and stood there beside me. He had killer eyes, huge, jaded, soul-sucking eyes, a nice and lazy smile, big thick lashes, and the lips of a real pervert.

Watching his face in profile, I'd felt faint at a sense of destiny between us—as though we were not standing beside each other in an elevator but were on the peaks of two separate and faraway mountains, with a deep valley and gorge between us. In that moment, I felt aware in my body of how difficult it would be to cross that distance to get to him.

As we stood there at the party, talking to each other up close, a trembling was going through me. I began to worry about my play—I had only just left my marriage and I needed to think about women, not men! I reminded myself, *The flower of love soon fades, but the flower of art is immortal!* But it was as if I was stuck to the floor beside him. When he asked me to leave the party, I startled myself by saying, "I'm celibate right now."

His eyes came alive in a different way, and his grin was the grin of a bear.

"So you're one of those people," he said.

"One of what people?"

"One of those people who think they can control themselves."

I blushed unhappily, then followed him out. I didn't want him to think I was one of those people who thought they could control themselves.

We walked together through the chilly night air for two or three hours, all the way down to the water. I felt, as we walked, *I could walk with you anywhere.* He noticed the shapes on buildings, other things I didn't see, pointing out this and that to me. He disagreed with me when I said you could love anyone. "No you can't," he said. "It matters—the person that you're with." I felt delight run through me and took pleasure in the excitement of just being near him.

We passed an ice cream truck, and he bought me an ice cream. Then we wandered back to his place, which was on the way to mine. I told myself that I was only walking him home, that I would leave him at his door so he could go in and change for his early shift at the bakery. But when we reached his place, I said, "I would like to watch you getting ready for work."

We went up the dark stairwell to the top of a run-down boardinghouse. He had two rooms at the top of the stairs: one for his drawing and painting, the other where he slept. He had no possessions other than a table, a mattress on the floor, a few dishes in the sink, and a hot plate plugged into the wall. I felt like I could just close my eyes and go to sleep on that mattress forever. There were no chairs, so I sat down on the messy sheets and watched him move around the room, then leave for the bathroom, then come back, showered and changed, coked up, his shirt open and untucked.

He got on the bed and put his hand on my thigh and rubbed it up and down, then got up and walked around the room and forgot what he was doing, then came back and kneeled beside me, and said into my ear, "I'll decide if you're celibate or not."

chapter 6

THE STORY OF THE *PUER*

Back at home, having walked Israel to the bakery, and having exchanged a hard and fluttering kiss, I went dizzily to sleep and had a dream: I was waiting at an airport. I was trying to get somewhere, to someplace higher and better. A bunch of people were at the airport too, and I was relieved and excited to see so many people I knew there. I went around getting their autographs.

I realized I had forgotten a bag at the other end of the terminal, so I ran, in a panic, to get it. An employee drove me back on a very slow buggy, and when I arrived at the gate, all the people who had been waiting were gone. I ran up to the counter and threw my two small tickets, desperately, into the flight attendant's hands. I begged to be let on—it was everything to me that I be let on!—but she said the plane had already left.

I spent days waiting for the next plane that was headed to where I wanted to go. I finally managed to board. Once again, there were people I knew there. I went to use the bathroom in the back, and the plane took off while I was sitting on the toilet. Though I knew the flight attendants would have been upset to find me there, I was happy because the view from the bathroom window was so amazing—we were flying so low to the city, just above the highways, flying in between the homes, dipping down sharply, then up. Then I realized this was not the way it was supposed to be, and I got scared.

We flew over a vast recycling center that only poor people used. Their bags of garbage went on forever. I was certain the plane would make an emergency landing there, but when it did not, I made a quick decision and slipped out the back door of the plane's bathroom. I landed safely on the ground, my fall softened by all the garbage bags.

I went into the recycling center—just a wooden shack surrounded by garbage, many miles from where we had taken off. Poor people were handing their garbage across the wood counter, and the man behind the counter was paying them pennies for it.

I went back outside and was surveying the dump when I noticed that my plane had crashed into a nearby lake. Its end was sticking out, smoking with fire. I was so relieved that I had jumped from the plane in time, but also spooked. I walked up to a curly-haired woman by the shore: my Jungian analyst. I asked her what the number of the flight

had been and she told me, but the numbers were not familiar. It had not been my plane at all!

Now my airplane was very far away—still traveling
through the sky! I would not be able to catch up to it by running or even with a car. I would have to find my way *back* to
the airport, *back* from this unfamiliar town, and take yet
another flight out.

I woke at four-thirty in the morning, my heart beating fast.
I had to discuss this dream with my Jungian analyst, so I
went to my computer and made it gently ring.

My analyst's name was Ann. She was in her midfifties.
Decades earlier, she had studied in Zurich, then moved to
Toronto where she practiced for many years. I met her
while I was studying at the university, taking her class on
Carl Jung. A few years later, I returned to her as a patient.
Two months ago, she moved to the English countryside to
live in a barn on a farm where her family had farmed for
generations, which was now idle and was where she had
been born.

I felt so grateful when she answered my call. It was
almost ten in the morning there. She asked me how I was;
if I'd had any dreams. I told her about my dream, and she
asked me if I had made any decisions lately. I couldn't think
of any, then I remembered my breakfast with Margaux and
my desire to pull the play.

Ann asked, "Did you imagine writing the play would

get you somewhere higher and better, just like an airplane does?"

I didn't know how to answer such a plainly obvious question. "Of course!"

"But then writing it turned out to be dangerous, like the airplane in your dream. So you've decided to quit. You slipped out of your marriage, too, which you also hoped would get you someplace higher and better."

SHEILA

(*defensive*) Wait! I want to cancel the play not because it's *dangerous*, but because life doesn't feel like it's in my stupid play, or with me sitting in a room *typing*. And life wasn't in my marriage anymore, either. Life feels like it's with Margaux—*talking*—which is an equally sincere attempt to get somewhere, just as sincere as writing a play.

Sheila sees Ann glance into the corner of her room.

ANN

But life isn't only where things are exciting; it's where things feel hard and stagnant, too. And arguing for a pure act that doesn't have a product in the end—well, there's two things there: one is there's not a concern for making a living; and second is there's not a concern with working to the end and winding up with something solid.

SHEILA

Except for the story of what happened.

ANN

The story of you talking to Margaux?

SHEILA

Perhaps.

Sheila becomes ashamed at the thought.

ANN

You slipped out from the plane at the first sign of danger, but then you returned to the airport to catch *another* plane? Why? Maybe there's a good reason to fear planes—one was weaving among the houses, the other one crashed. You could have *walked* from the dump. What's wrong with walking? It might take much longer . . . forty years as opposed to four hours. But you're more likely to arrive there, safely.

I couldn't help the sudden, hard laugh that came from my mouth. It seemed too simple—a fantasy! I tried to cover up the fact that I had laughed.

ANN

There's taking airplanes and waiting for airplanes, but another possibility is to make the difficult choices and decide. You remember the *puer aeternus*—the eternal child—Peter Pan—the boy who never grows up, who never becomes a man? Or it's like in *The Little Prince*—when the prince asks the narrator to draw him a sheep. The narrator tries and tries again, but each time he fails to do it as well as he wishes.

He believes himself to be a great artist and cannot understand why it's not working. In a fit of frustration, he instead draws a box—something he *can* do well. When the prince asks how it's a picture of a sheep, the narrator replies that it's a picture of a sheep in a box. He is arrogantly proud of his solution and satisfied with his efforts. This response is typical of all *puers*. Such people will suddenly tell you they have another plan, and they always do it the moment things start getting difficult. But it's their everlasting switching that's the dangerous thing, not what they choose.

Sheila's heart beats up in her chest . . .

SHEILA

Why is their everlasting switching dangerous?

ANN

Because people who live their lives this way can look forward to a single destiny, shared with others of this type— though such people do not believe they represent a *type*, but feel themselves distinguished from the common run of man, who they see as held down by the banal anchors of the world. But while others actually build a life in which things gain in meaning and significance, this is not true of the *puer*. Such a person inevitably looks back on life as it nears its end with a feeling of emptiness and sadness, aware of what they have built: nothing. In their quest for a life without failure, suffering, or doubt, that is what they achieve: a life empty of all those things that make a human life meaningful. And yet they started off believing themselves too special for this world!

. . . Sheila listens on, in agony, fear, and dread . . .

But—and here is the hope—there *is* a solution for people of this type, and it's perhaps not the solution that could have been predicted. The answer for them is to build on what they have begun and not abandon their plans as soon as things start getting difficult. They must *work*—without escaping into fantasies about being *the person who worked.* And I don't mean work for its own sake, but they must choose work that begins and ends in a passion, a question that is gnawing at their guts, which is not to be avoided but must be realized and lived through the hard work and suffering that inevitably comes with the process.

. . . Sheila's insides begin to tremble . . .

They must reinforce and build on what is in their life already rather than always starting anew, hoping to find a situation without danger. *Puers* don't need to check themselves into analysis. If they can just remember this—*It is their everlasting switching that is the dangerous thing, not what they choose*—they might discover themselves saved. The problem is the *puer* ever anticipates loss, disappointment, and suffering— which they foresee at the end of every experience, so they cut themselves off at the beginning, retreating almost at once in order to protect themselves. In this way, they never give themselves to life—living in constant dread of the end. Reason, in this case, has taken too much from life.

. . . a weak personality . . . who only wishes to avoid suffering!

They must give themselves completely to the experience! One thinks sometimes how much more alive such people would be if they suffered! If they can't be happy, let them at least be unhappy—really, really unhappy for once, and then they might become truly human.

I fell back, exhausted.

If I can do this, then perhaps my life, when I look back on it, will at least be not as empty as the heart of any Casanova.

· *chapter 7* ·

PRAYER OF THE *PUER*

There's so much beauty in this world that it's hard to begin. There are no words with which to express my gratitude at having been given this one chance to live—if not *Live*. Let other people frequent the nightclubs in their tight-ass skirts and *Live*. I'm just sitting here, vibrating in my apartment, at having been given this one chance to live.

I am writing a play. I am writing a play that is going to save the world. If it only saves three people, I will not be happy. If with this play the oil crisis is merely averted and our standard of living maintains itself at its current level, I will weep into my oatmeal. If this play does anything short of announcing the arrival of the next cock—I mean, messiah—I will shit into my oatmeal.

Who among us will be asked to lead the people out of bondage, only to say, *God, I have never been a good talker. Ask someone else. Ask my brother instead of me.* There is no way to accomplish what I feel I must accomplish with this play. There is no way in heaven or on earth! I am the wrong person to do it. Look at the shitty red hoodie I am sitting here in. Look at my dirty running shoes. I have such small breasts. God, shouldn't you call upon a woman with great big knockers, who the people will listen to? Why do you call on me, who doesn't have the cleavage to capture the world's attention? Ask my sister instead of me, whose big breasts are much more suited to doing your work.

May the Lord have mercy on me for I am a fucking idiot. But I live in a culture of fucking idiots. I cannot be saved if not everyone is saved. If everyone around me talks nothing but shit, how can I hold myself aloof? My fate is not separate from everyone's fate. If one man or one woman can stand up and call themselfs saved, that means we all are. And I know I'm not, so no one is.

Last night someone said to me, "Come on—all the five, six times I have seen you, you have been drunk out of your mind." I was drunk last night too, when he was telling it to me. I resented the implication that I had been, in the five, six times we had seen each other, any drunker than he had been. For we are all, all of us, drunk all the time, and it's not fair for him to single me out like that and make me the exception, when if it comes to the drinking habits in the circles I run in, I am the rule. The rule is: drink as much as you can afford to drink. We all, anyway, work better when we are drunk, or wake up the next morning, hungover. In either case, we lack the capacity to second-guess ourselves.

People say there is no direction to evolution—upward to any height; that the proper metaphor is the outward webbing of a bush, not the striving of a tree toward the heavens. When we were children, we would lift our arms to the skies as high as we could—as tall as we could make ourselves—*stretch, stretch, stretch!* When I look back on those gym classes and how we all stretched ourselves to be as tall as the tallest tree, I can't help but think, *Those were the most religious moments of my life.*

If now in some ways I drink too much, it's not that I lack a reverence for the world.

Today I am fasting. A girl I know who is a semifamous singer, and who is very slender and glamorous in pictures, once told me that when she has been eating badly, she will fast for a day or two. She said that Nietzsche made her think that her self-denial and need for purification were vulgar bullshit, but then she said no to Nietzsche—she sees no reason she shouldn't enjoy emptying out, the same as she enjoys exploiting abundance.

The other night out at the bars, I learned that Nietzsche wrote on a typewriter. It is unbelievable to me, and I no longer feel that his philosophy has the same validity or aura of truth that it formerly did. No other detail of his life situating him so squarely in the modern age could have affected me as much as learning this. He *typed Zarathustra*? Goddamnit, the man had no more connection to the truth than a stenographer!

Knowing this, I don't see why I don't just kick it all to hell and shut up at last about my concern that I might put more shit into the world. The world is full to brimming with its own shit. A little more from me won't even make a difference—it's only natural. It's to be expected. I should put a lot of shit in the play, so it will be a multicolored shit.

Everyone enjoys economy for its relation to a certain morality, but if I have to suffer from other people's excesses, why should I not suffer doubly from my own?

chapter 8

MARGAUX PAINTS

I worked on my play for several days, badly. Finally one night, needing to get out of my apartment, I picked up my computer and went with it to our studio. It was early on a Friday evening, and I was walking slowly when I heard someone call out my name.

I turned and saw Margaux coming down the alley. She was pushing something on a trolley in front of her, and as she got closer I saw it was a tree—a baby tree in a pot! We hugged hello, and then I asked her if it was a tree she had grown. She said it was. Margaux grew plants on her balcony and she was really good at getting them strong. I was curious to know what her secret was. She told me she was going now to plant the tree in a friend's yard, a friend whose father had recently died. I decided to go with her, and as we walked together, we talked.

SHEILA

You know what? If we ever have kids, I really like the idea of trading babies.

MARGAUX

(*laughing*) Yeah, that'd be fun—getting pregnant together. And you're right! We'd have such adoring love for each other's baby. But it might be hard . . .

SHEILA

What? To give up your own?

MARGAUX

Maybe . . . Do you think you'd prefer one to the other?

SHEILA

I think I'd have more fun if it was yours.

MARGAUX

Yeah, exactly, you would!

Laughter.

I think it's a great idea. I think I always want culture to work like that. I think it would be less emotionally compli-cated if I was raising society's child. But you'd have to sleep with somebody who's really big with black hair.

SHEILA

No, because babies can be anything.

MARGAUX

But when they turn twenty, boy!

They laugh.

When we got to the yard, I watched as she dug a neat, deep hole and placed the tree inside it. I leaned against the fence and waited until she was done. I said I would walk her home, but on the way to her apartment, we stopped in at my place so I could pick up a sweater. Inside, Margaux pointed to a pile of papers on my desk, which were labelled on top with a black marker, *Margaux*.

"What's that?" she asked.

"Our conversations," I said.

Margaux was quiet. She went to wait by the stairs.

On the walk to her place, Margaux mentioned that she had been painting swimming pools. In every painting she had made that month, there was a pool. She said she had been working on a painting of *me* in a pool before she left her house that night, based on the naked photos she had taken of me in the whirlpool at the Y. Did I want to see it? Of course I did! All my life I had dreamed of being friends with a painter who would make me into an icon that people would admire.

In her painting studio we stood before her fresh canvases. I recognized my narrow body in a small angular pool, seemingly outdoors, my head wooden and stiff. She put on the prescription glasses I had given her, without which she couldn't see. I had told her, when I gave them to her, that it might be nice for her to see her paintings. She said she had never considered it, the images coming directly from inside her head.

Now she explained, touching its sides, "I wanted to call it *The Genius* but instead I'm calling it *House for a Head*. I don't believe enough in genius, but I *do* believe in having a house for a head."

I almost cried. I didn't want to say it, but I felt pretty crummy at being demoted from *genius* to simply having a house for a head.

Alone in our studio, sitting before my computer, I was determined to finish my play, but instead I grew distracted and stared out the window. I now saw that hanging out with Margaux, and talking with Margaux, and sharing a studio with Margaux was not enough to make me a genius in the world. It would not help me lead the people or make me into the sort of person I should be. It would not help me finish my play, or solve any of my problems.

Yes it would. It would solve them all.

chapter 9

THEY WANDER IN MIAMI

That winter, Margaux's gallerist decided to take some of her paintings to Miami, where for a week the city would be turned into a giant art fair. Collectors from all over the world would attend, and all the top galleries would be there. The fanciest art would be shown at Art Basel, the largest of the fairs, and of the smaller fairs orbiting its periphery, one, called Scope, was where Margaux's work would be.

Though her dealer had already left for Florida, Margaux continued painting. I said she should deliver the newest paintings by hand, not ship them, and said it was important for me to take the trip down with her. I wanted to record us there. Didn't I need to write my play? she asked. I told her that the trip would be like writing; I hoped that if we went away together, like the mothers in my play, I could later study the transcripts and figure out what reality had that my play did not; learn why my play was not working, which was maybe the same reason my character was not working, and thus discover how I and the play should be.

Then I watched, the morning we were to board public transit to the airport, as Margaux stuffed three oil paintings packed in bubble wrap into her large duffel bag, along with twenty T-shirts. We were only going for three days.

On the plane ride down, we read an article in the *New York Times* about a painter who would be attending the fair that week, a twenty-five-year-old guy named Ted Mineo who had studied at Yale and was being represented by one of the top Soho galleries. Basel would be his debutante ball. From Miami Basel to the heavens! His dealer intended him to meet everyone. No doubt he would be kept busy his entire time there. It read as though his life for the past five years had been very well managed, from art school, to his discovery in art school, to his move to Brooklyn and so on, so he was quoted saying of the contemporary art world, "There's a career track. You get your B.F.A. and then you get your M.F.A. You move to New York, you have a show, and it's like being a lawyer or something else. And that doesn't entirely square with the romantic ideal of being an artist, living in isolation and being the avant-garde hero."

When we finished reading it, I asked Margaux if she had ever thought about going to Yale. She told me she had once spent several weeks thinking about it, after searching around on the internet and realizing that all the big artists had gone there. She had made millions of sacrifices for her art—maybe she should beg, borrow, and steal whatever she could to go. But then she thought, *No, that's awful*—because there were just too many people who could not, and it seemed like it shouldn't be the rule that you have to attend Yale. "In the end," she said, "it felt too unfair to even think about, and it just seemed wrong to my morals and my faith in art. I think it would have really hurt me and made me sad. To me, it looked the same as joining a country club that Jews or black people aren't allowed into. And lots of good people *do* join country clubs. But it would depress me too much. I figured I had to see what would happen without me joining the country club."

When we arrived in Miami, we changed from our pants and sweaters, getting half-naked in the airport washroom, our clothes spread all over the counters. "Be careful," I told Margaux, since she was so loyal. "Whatever outfit you choose for yourself now, you'll be wearing for the next three days."

Recently, Margaux had been trying to reassure me that I had a good brain. My brain had not worried me when I was younger, but over the past year I had become convinced that I did not think as well as other people. No, that was putting it gently—that I didn't know how to think at all. Other people knew how to think, I thought, had opinions on things, a point of view. I did not.

As we walked down the side of the Miami highway, my arm linked through hers, the crescent moon faint in the sky

overhead, I again brought up my fear. I explained that I felt
my insides were a blank—a total neutrality—null.

"That's amazing!" she said. "*God,* everyone else is like
these automatic windup toys."

"But I feel like other people are seeing and perceiving
and synthesizing, and I'm—I'm not doing any of that!"

"You're doing something, boy, let me tell you. I think
mainly people have opinions on, *Well, what do you think
about abortion?* Everybody we hang out with is pretty com-
petent at vaguely intelligent party talk, but you say things
that help me think better, you know?"

I shrugged, but inside was filled with something new,
and prayed that what she said was true.

In any case, I believed it to be gold and held it near.

We finally found a cab and took Margaux's paintings to
Scope—a large, makeshift tent in the center of a muddy
field in a park, in what the taxi driver told us was a very bad
neighborhood that the city was trying to fix with art. Having delivered her paintings, we got into another taxi, then
dropped our bags at our cookie-cutter hotel. We hoped to
get dinner in Little Havana, at the other end of town, and
walked around for a while trying to find a bus stop.

At four o'clock, we stepped onto a bus, midway through
a conversation about what you need to know in writing
and what you need to know in art. We came to the same
conclusion: you have to know where the funny is, and if
you know where the funny is, you know everything. Sit-

ting up front, across from a seat labeled *IN MEMORY OF ROSA PARKS*, we tested out this theory.

MARGAUX

David Lynch is pretty funny.

SHEILA

And Harmony Korine is hysterical. And do you think Werner Herzog is hysterical?

MARGAUX

(*laughing*) Oh my God, yeah. He's really funny in a Kafka kind of way.

SHEILA

I think Manet is funny.

MARGAUX

Yeah, Manet is very funny.

SHEILA

And Kierkegaard is really funny.

MARGAUX

Really? I see him as so sweet. I see him so much more like poetry.

SHEILA

Do you think Nietzsche's funny?

MARGAUX

I haven't read him much. Baudrillard?

SHEILA

Haven't read him enou—hmm. Richard Serra's not funny.

MARGAUX

No. He seems to take himself and art *very* seriously. It's nice to take it seriously while also leaving your back door open. I mean, your pants down.

SHEILA

(*laughing*) You mean slipping on a banana peel.

MARGAUX

You know, I didn't realize that you—you can't really slip on a banana peel unless it's rotten. Which is what happened to me.

SHEILA

Was the buttery side down?

MARGAUX

It was all black, so it was hard to tell.

SHEILA

(*laughs*) How about Jackson Pollock?

MARGAUX

Not funny.

SHEILA

Mark Rothko?

MARGAUX

I mean, all those guys are—I mean, one of them would have been enough for me.

After finishing our dinner, we returned to Scope and arrived just as it was closing. A tall, aloofly handsome Asian man blithely dragged behind him a cabbage on a leash, making his way into and out of the rooms. People noticed, but no one cared. Since the lights were going down, we walked superfast through all the booths: *like it . . . hate it . . . don't like it . . . don't care . . .* then walked out through the doors and into the night after pausing briefly to say hello to a pale, thin, blond Chelsea dealer we both knew.

Leaving the tent, Margaux began to rage. "Of course! She leans in to kiss you, but she doesn't kiss me. Connecticut! All the Connecticut bitches hate me!" To calm her from the slight, I asked her to recite what I knew to be her favorite American poem—Matt Cook's poem.

"Okay. 'James Joyce . . .'" I prompted.

MARGAUX

(*sighs*)

James Joyce
He was stupid
He didn't know as much as me
I'd rather throw dead batteries at cows
Than read him
Everything was going fine
Before he came along
He started the Civil War
He tried to get the French involved
But they wouldn't listen
They filled him up with desserts
He talked about all the great boxers
That came from Ireland
Like he trained 'em or something
Then he started reading some of his stuff
Right as we told him to get lost
He brought up the potato famine
We said "Your potatoes are plenty good.
Deal with it! Work it out somehow."
Then he said "America must adopt the metric system.
It's much more logical." We said "No!
We like our rulers! Go away!"
Thomas Jefferson said, "You always get the rulers you
    deserve."

SHEILA

Do you know any other poems by heart?

MARGAUX

No.

We sat down on the pavement and waited forty-five minutes for a cab to take us to the beach where the city was
hosting a Peaches concert. I pulled out my tape recorder—
Margaux glanced down at it—and we began to discuss
Margaux's hopes for the fair. I couldn't understand how anyone could get famous in a place like this, where there were
thousands of artists and so many galleries, and all of the art
just laid out to speak for itself like cereal boxes on super-
market shelves, but without even the words. The art and the
artists had started blurring together for me, and I suggested
that as yet we had seen nobody truly great.

MARGAUX

Well, *of course* there are people here that are really truly
great! But how could you see that? Like, for instance, if
Takashi Murakami had just one of his sculptures here, you
wouldn't know how good it was.

SHEILA

You don't think?

MARGAUX

No! But both of us have read these extensive articles about
him. Like, of course if you saw *one piece* by Takashi Murakami—
but we have such nuances because of articles and context and

because we've seen his past work and, you know. But this is so many young artists trying to show all of that in one go.

SHEILA

So the point here is not to decide who's the greatest artist?

MARGAUX

Not at all. Not at all. But it *is* a chance to let the younger artists in. It *is* a chance to let the smaller galleries in. I don't know what it is. It's not everything.

SHEILA

If you think that going to an art fair and having your pictures in a booth will make you famous, it won't.

MARGAUX

But no one's thinking that at all!

SHEILA

Hmm. I would be thinking that if *I* was an artist here.

Then we went to the concert and got into a fight after I told Margaux, "All the art you like is only *almost* good." In bad moods, we met up with her dealer and walked in the rain to get some food, and went into a pizza place and sat by the window. Margaux ordered a Hawaiian slice. As we were eating, a boy and girl in their early twenties who were obviously part of the art crowd came in and addressed Margaux directly.

"Are you Margaux Williamson?" the girl asked excitedly.

"Yes," Margaux replied.

"Oh my God, I love your paintings! I've seen them on the internet!"

We looked at each other, wide-eyed.

The boy added, "I met you at an art fair in Los Angeles! I'm a painter too."

As they went on to talk about her work, my mind went to a video Margaux had made of our friend Ryan's performance of a song he had written for his band, Tomboyfriend. She put it on YouTube, and one viewer listed himself as a fan; a man, supposedly, from Afghanistan. Planning the band's first concert, Margaux had carefully chosen the title: *Big in Afghanistan*.

That night, back at the hotel, Margaux and I lay in one of the beds and watched as, on my computer, an heiress gave her boyfriend a hand job. She seemed really into it; there was no reason to doubt it. Then her cell phone rang, and she let go of his dick and threw her body across the bed and answered with a far more convincing show of enthusiasm than she had shown while jiggling his cock. Her boyfriend was scowling now. After fifteen seconds, he said, "Get off your fucking phone." She talked a moment more, then hung up and returned to where she had left off.

She was an eerie figure who appeared in the pale gray outlines of night vision. Her eyes glowed like the eyes of a cat. Watching her, I felt a kinship; she was just another white girl going through life with her clothes off. I told

myself quietly, *Consider all the warriors down through time,
without great brains—like you!—who nevertheless struck the
enemy right through the breast. They just kept their wrists steady
and struck.*

Then I glanced at the painting of the Statue of Liberty
on the wall behind us and wondered, *Where would all of
America be—and wouldn't the flame long be extinguished in the
sea—if not for that tall girl's steady wrist?*

MARGAUX

You know, this video totally reminds me of once when I
was at a party in Texas. I was about thirteen years old, and
there was this girl there who was getting pissed on by these
two guys. And she really was the most lost girl.

SHEILA

Oh.

MARGAUX

I just wish that she had a bit of what this girl has—her freedom, her shamelessness.

Pause.

You know, sometimes I get really excited thinking about
autism. I think, *Oh! Over there in Silicon Valley there are all
these kids with autism . . .* and I think maybe it's an advanta-
geous human trait. Maybe it's sort of wonderful to—

SHEILA

—to lack feelings?

MARGAUX

To lack an overwhelming empathy. I sometimes feel pretty paralyzed by my own feelings of empathy. And it's still such a problem—shame. Maybe what I want in my life is to cut out a bit of the empathy and a bit of the shame.

The next morning, we lay on the beach for several hours, then swam so far out to sea that a lifeguard in his motorized vehicle had to drive onto the beach and blow his whistle to get us to come back to shore, while everyone stared. We dried ourselves off in the sand and went to see our final fair of the trip, Art Basel, which we had to line up for and pay twenty dollars to get into. Standing in the cold, cavernous, convention-center air, we picked up a full-color map to help find our way around. There were coffee kiosks everywhere in case visitors grew weary, and it was at Art Basel that we found the wealthiest patrons and the most expensive art. The fair was being sponsored by a bank. On the banners hung outside the building and in the corridors leading into the rooms where the panel discussions and the temporary bookstores were, was this message: *USB welcomes you to Art Basel Miami Beach*. Below it was a quote from Andy Warhol: *Everybody's sense of beauty is different from everybody else's.*

I asked Margaux what she thought the quote meant. Glancing at it, she grimaced. "Oh yeah. It's saying you can be rich and stupid about art. You're all welcome."

Several hours later, growing tired from the art and the cold, we left. Out in front, at the bottom of a short flight of stairs, a young woman sat staring off into infinity, slowly winding a ball of string around her body and the handrails. We paused to glance at her, then walked off into the streets, where every one of the houses was painted a different pastel color: pink, yellow, orange, green, blue.

Then I heard my friend say calmly, "I don't care about success. I have it in my heart now."

After the sun went down, Margaux and I went strolling through the big, fluorescent-lit shops. We bought the same yellow dress, then met up with Cappy, who was down with his shipping business, not with his own paintings, as in the past.

Now the three of us were walking through the streets, along with all the women in their tight skirts and cleavage and tans and makeup and high heels, who were holding on to their big, bulky boyfriends for balance.

Cappy led us through the baronial doors of a fancy blue hotel, and we went out to the back where there was a giant pool and very elegant people sitting at long tables, eating salmon and steak and drinking lots of wine. We sat on a half-wall at a short distance from everyone. Cappy and Margaux began saying they were hungry. "Hold on," I said, excitedly, and I pretended to be a waiter, and took the neglected plates and goblets away from the patrons and delivered them to Margaux and Cappy; we drank the half-drunk wine and ate up all the leftovers.

"So, Margaux," asked Cappy, chewing, "have any of your paintings sold?"

"I don't know," she said. "I don't think so. Maybe. I haven't asked."

Then we went for a stroll along the beach and ran into an old rich couple and struck up a conversation. The woman began talking about how they were thinking of buying a twenty-three-thousand-dollar Ruscha print, having just come from dinner with the gallerist who was selling it. Their collection included a Gerhard Richter, and they had so little wall space left that whatever they bought in Miami would end up *in rotation*.

MARGAUX

That's all I hear from collectors.

CAPPY

They take something down, and then they hang the new thing.

WOMAN

We do that, but we don't sell it.

SHEILA

Yeah, because you love it.

WOMAN

We rotate it.

MARGAUX

You know, I think it's really good for artists to come here and see this.

WOMAN

To show that there's a lot of great art out there?

MARGAUX

And to know that it's not important.

WOMAN

What's not important?

MARGAUX

This.

As we were talking, my phone rang and I answered it. I recognized the lazy voice and at once felt faint, and I moved away from my friends. "Are you having a good time?" Israel asked. I said that I was. I tried to explain that we were talking to some rich people. "Would you like to have my cum in your mouth right now, talking to those rich people? That would be pretty good, wouldn't it?" Not knowing what else to say, I stammered, "Yes." When I got off the phone, I made a new rule for myself: that I would never again take his call—or, anyway, not until I finished my play—so never.

Returning to Margaux and Cappy, feeling sensitive, I noticed Margaux's face as she talked to the rich lady. She looked as she always did when she could find no value in a person—an expression so apparent to me, and so painful, for I was sure the rich people could see it, too—a hard, quick look of boredom and dismissal. I felt afraid whenever I saw it, worried that one day she would turn it on me. Coming near, I heard the woman say that it was not *necessary* for them to buy, but if they saw something they liked, they had the *ability* to buy, "though it's not like we have zillions of dollars."

As we walked off, Margaux said, "Sure, she has so much money that she has to make up an amount of money that doesn't exist to say how much money she *doesn't* have."

I needed another drink, so we went back to the hotel and drank. Then I said, "Let's get naked and jump in the pool." So we stripped down to our underwear and got in the pool. We were the only ones swimming. Fifteen minutes later, tiring of the pool, I beckoned to a man who was sitting nearby. "We need towels!" I cried, and he waved down a hotel man and collected three fluffy towels for us. We swam to the edge, thanking him as we got out. The man smiled and replied, "No problem." It was Keanu Reeves! Margaux moved slowly away, but I hung back and talked a bit, then Margaux and I left.

Margaux grows very embarrassed as they walk away.

MARGAUX

Oh, *God*! I really wish we had seen a really more famous, more annoying celebrity! I wish we had seen a celebrity I don't actually defend in public! But I like his work! I seriously have on my profile, like, Werner Herzog, Laurie Anderson, Gertrude Stein, and Keanu Reeves!

SHEILA

Really?

MARGAUX

Yes! Ugh! I just wish that all the people I liked were either my best friends or total strangers. As they are, of course, but . . .

We stumbled into a cab and took it the six blocks to our hotel and went up the elevator into our room. In three hours, we would have to get up and fly home. As I stood by the sink, trying to wash from my favorite white dress the red wine we had spilled on it earlier that night, I chatted brightly.

SHEILA

I'm so happy with how we were making everyone jealous with how happy we were in the pool!

MARGAUX

What? That's *crazy!* In my mind, we were making *ourselves* happy. I had no idea anyone was looking at us.

SHEILA

All I'm saying is: if there's a pool and people are in the pool and you're not in the pool, you want to be in the pool just like those people in the pool. It's just a fact of nature.

Sheila gets into the bed they are sharing.

MARGAUX

Hehe. You have no underpants on.

SHEILA

I don't mind. I don't object.

MARGAUX

I thought maybe you didn't know.

SHEILA

I *realize*.

I immediately passed out but I forgot to shut down the tape recorder. After ten minutes, Margaux can be heard asking me, *Are you awake?* I wasn't, but I gave a little grunt to show that I was. Then Margaux said softly, perhaps half-asleep herself: *I feel like either it's a dream, or it's some kid I know from Texas, like this black kid, nice kid, smart kid, and he just—he just wanted . . . he hated all the football games, but he really liked the part when we were winning. And he would just make the T-shirts from whenever we were winning . . . and he would make everything from when we were winning.*

After a twenty-second pause, she spoke again: *He really wasn't interested in the game.*

And after a thirty-second pause: *So everybody got mad at him.*

Then Margaux fell asleep, and after several minutes of silence, the tape recorder shut itself off.

chapter 10

TWO DRESSES

A week back in Toronto, Sheila receives an email from Margaux . . .

1. i know i can be intense sometimes, and i know you have a lot going on, and this is not that big of a deal, but i wanted to say that it really startled me in miami when you bought the same yellow dress that i was buying.

2. after we looked at a thousand dresses for you—and the yellow dress being the first dress i was considering—i really was surprised when you said you were getting it too.

3. i suggested you try it on when i thought there was only one size, but when you said you were also getting it, i didn't know what to say or think.

4. i think it's pretty standard that you don't buy the

dress your friend is buying, but i was trying to convince myself that maybe it was okay to buy the same dress your friend is buying. you know, trying to think about it positively, hence the "we'll wear them in our music video" statement from me.

5. when you said that you'd only wear it out of town and never in toronto, it sort of seemed reasonable.

6. but not really, since of course we only exist in pictures.

7. i should have been clearer in the store about how it made me uncomfortable, or i just shouldn't have bought the dress.

8. i really do need some of my own identity. and this is pretty simple and good for the head.

9. i'm going to get rid of the dress now, cause it makes me a little sad to look at it.

10. you don't have to reply to this email.

Hurt and shocked, I did not.

INTERLUDE FOR FUCKING

That morning, as I was getting dressed, I fastened behind my back a lacy pink push-up bra and pulled out from the drawer a nice pink pair of panties. The underpants suited the bra beautifully, and I smiled at this, but then I thought, *No wait, Israel said he wants to see you tomorrow, save the pink panties for tomorrow.* I hesitated back and forth, then decided to put on the pink panties, since I had no intention of seeing Israel tomorrow, or on any other day. I would never let him see my underpants, and wanted to remind myself of this.

The day went on, and at around noon I got a call. Israel had emailed after we spoke in Miami, saying he would call me on Saturday to make plans. I had not replied. It was only Friday, so it took me a moment to realize it was him. Then I understood that he had been thinking about me and just couldn't wait. My heart started beating fast. I didn't know what to do, so I told him I would call him back. I closed up the phone, unable to eat another piece of sushi, but I forced myself to put one more piece in my mouth, then I paid the young woman and left. I started walking south, taking me at once closer to my home and to where I knew he lived.

Just moments before, sitting at the Japanese restaurant, I had been leafing through the pages of the *I Ching*, which I had bought right before lunch. I hoped the book would teach me something about how to be, and had randomly opened to a page that read: "RENUNCIATION: Voluntary retreat brings good fortune to the superior man, and downfall to the inferior man."

Walking now, and thinking it through, I saw the book was right. The only way to be faithful to my ideal of celibacy and thus finish my play would be to retreat. I would call Israel and tell him that I could not see him until July, seven months from now, which is when I believed I would be finished with it and ready to come out of my celibacy and think about men once more. I smiled and felt relieved at this plan. For the first time on my walk, I noticed what a lovely winter day it was; how everything was covered in soft white snow. My decision made me cheerful. I had no need of any man.

With new vigor and confidence and delight, I called him back. I said I couldn't see him the next day, but I would see him in July, when I would be ready. I told him all of this as I walked. I explained that he had gotten under my skin, and that I really did like him, but these feelings were not working with my plan. If I saw him, I would fall deeper into things, so I had to resist. I had never before spoken to a man in such a way—admitting absolutely everything.

I felt calm and true until he said, "That is the most pretentious thing I have ever heard. Don't you believe in the moment? Who knows where anyone will be in July?"

I understood at once what he meant. If I did not see him today, by July there would be another girl. Perhaps it would be the girl he would marry.

"All right," I said. "I can't see you tomorrow night, but I'll meet you right now, for a walk."

He was pleased. We agreed on the corner where we'd meet, and I rehearsed in my head what I would say when I saw him: *Sorry, all signs point to renunciation.* But when I saw him coming down the street, I only smiled at his thick black lashes, at his big brown eyes, his slimness, his pink lips. I didn't mention renunciation once.

We spent three or four hours walking, making our way down to the water. We passed a group of schoolchildren, and when a little boy ran into him and jumped away scared, Israel raised his hands, laughing. I said to myself, *He's a good man.*

He told me about how, over the past year, he had thought about me often. He had a friend who rented a studio on the second floor of Katharine's gallery, right beside the room Margaux and I shared. When he went to meet his friend he'd sometimes see us sitting there, quietly working. He told me, "I thought about taking those flowers from your desk, just stuffing them in your mouth, and bending you over the desk and fucking you."

They weren't flowers but mint leaves—a present from Margaux—but I did not say so.

We went into an alley, and with one hand he held my waist and with the other he pulled down the front of my jeans, slightly, as if to have a glance.

"These are pretty panties," he said.

All right, Israel, cum in my mouth. Don't let me wash it out, so when I talk to those people, I can have your cum swimming in my mouth, and I will smile at them and taste you. It will be as you wanted it, me standing there, tasting your cum, stumbling over my words. And if you see something you don't like, you can correct me later. You can take your hands and bruise my neck, keep pushing till you feel the soft flesh at the back of my throat, so the tears roll down my cheeks like they do every time you thrust your cock to the very back of my throat—like it never was with any other man. I never always had tears rolling down my face. Even when you hear me gagging you don't stop. It's your unconcern that makes me want you to do whatever you want with my body, which can be for you, while yours cannot be for me. I can see that your body must be for many women, and though I once thought the same of mine— that mine must be for all the men who wanted me—I can just tease with it if you will keep on fucking me. I wouldn't want your cum wasted on just one girl, not when there are so many girls to take your disinterested thrusting. Fuck whichever sluts it's your fancy to fuck. You will find me in our home one day, cooking or doing your laundry, as you wish, washing your slutty underwear that some girl slutted on while you were out. I'll make you your meals and serve you them, leave you alone to paint while I go into my room. Then in the morning when we wake, you can look down, touch your cock. It's hard. Do you need me then? Tell me, as you did the first time I woke in your bed, *I like to have my cock sucked in the morning.*

All right, Israel. I will put it in my mouth. You just close your eyes. I will do my work for you in the morning.

I don't know why all of you just sit in libraries when you could be fucked by Israel. I don't know why all of you are reading books when you could be getting reamed by Israel, spat on, beaten up against the headboard—with every jab, your head battered into the headboard. Why are you all reading? I don't understand this reading business when there is so much fucking to be done.

It always starts off the same, easy; you just get into bed. But instead of picking up a book, you have Israel there, so no moments pass before his soft flesh is on your flesh, and his hands are on your skin like it's your skin—not some alien skin but your skin moving from the inside.

What is there in that book anyway? What is there to be learned tonight when you could learn to suck Israel's cock? What is there to think about when your brains could so easily be smashed against the headboard, in which case there's no way to think of anything?

I don't see what you're getting so excited about, snuggling in with your book, you little bookworms, when instead Israel could be stuffing his cock into you and teaching you a lesson, pulling down your arms, adjusting your face so he can see it, stuffing your hand into your mouth, and fucking your brains right out of your head.

I don't see why you walk down the street so easily, not noticing that you are living half a life—or how you move up to the counter to order a tuna sandwich like there is nothing else in the world—when there is only *one* thing in the world to be paying attention to right now, which is that you are not getting your brains fucked out of your skull by Israel, and don't you think that's a problem, you stupid, brain-dead slut?

I'm just saying—because I was watching you there and I thought, *This stupid fucking know-nothing slut needs her brains scrambled by the cock of Israel. Her throat has never been bruised down its back by him*—is all I was thinking when I saw you ordering your sandwich. *Tuna fish*, lady? Do you have no dignity? Is your body a limp half-body? Or is it impossible to have any dignity unless you are getting nightly reamed by Israel?

If you would like to call your mother, go and do it. The sun is shining, it's half past noon, the time for tears is now. Please tell her I said hello and that I think her daughter's a stupid cunt if she thinks she can go around the world with her priss-ass high in the air like a queen on a throne while not having known the humiliation of being fucked by Israel.

It is afternoon. It is evening. All the people are going to sleep except Israel, who is a working man—but sleep has no friendship with him this week—whose sleep is being slaughtered and slit.

I really must hand it to all the grocers in this town, to all the flower sellers, all the pastry makers, all the people who stand on the floor of the stock exchange with their computers and their ticker tape—the secretaries, the office lunchers who sit in dreary underground malls and eat their lunches—their grungy Chinese noodles, their grungy ham and cheese— who have no joy, who have no fucking, who have nothing but the dreariness of having never been fucked by Israel.

It's Sunday now for all you lonely fuckers, but for me it's always Sunday afternoon. There is nothing but Sundays and three in the afternoons for me now—and even midnight is as leisurely as a stroll, all the leisure of being battered and bashed by Israel. You poor beautiful lonely suckers whose lives I never wept for until now, whose sorrow I never noticed until now, whose dreariness I never dreamed of till now, till now. Enjoy what you can of a life without the magnificent cock of Israel.

. . .

Then love, which can't be helped, slips into the death drive. The death drive seeks comfort and knowledge of the future. It wants the final answer and is afraid of life. It is weary of life. It is weary of self-containment, the continuation of its purpose, the channeling of the energies of the self. It wants to step into the oblivion of someone else, and its heart races at annihilation. It renounces and gives up renouncing equally. Cliffs are the friend of the death drive, particularly cliffs into another person. It wants a mutual plummeting into the center, one into the other, like a sixty-nine. It hopes to drive you off your course like a car plunging into the center of the earth. It strives for love, annihilation, comfort, and death. *Now the future is clear!* it cries. It wants to drag you down.

But if you lie still, you may find that you want to lie there in bed beside him not because of the death drive, but for a different reason, which is that you are enjoying looking at his beautiful green-walled room and being alive— the sun coming in with the breeze, and the drawings on the wall tacked up with clear tacks and green tacks and yellow and blue, and it is not even so much about the man beside you in the bed, but what a room, what a room!

Then, when your heart sinks again, it sinks from the death drive like a serpent creeping in—but from another direction this time; so you thought you had closed up all the stops, but you missed this one. You missed it, and the serpent slithered in. It is death coming, masquerading as life, and blessed is the man who can see the death drive in the woman. Blessed is he who leaves in the morning without any promise of love. And blessed is the woman who can answer for herself, What about *living*? What is it about *living* that you want?

In the mornings, he would get up from the bed and leave. I never saw any sentiment in his eyes. He would roll up the sleeves of his shirt so slowly. Watching him dress, the careful way he did it, and how his underwear came up over the lip of his jeans, I knew he could never be mine. That casual way of dressing before a woman, slowly and deliberately, with so much attention paid to every little gesture of grooming—though he told me that a man must never dress any better than the woman he is with.

Israel, if you ever want a child, I don't want to talk about it. I don't want to sit around the table and discuss the whens and ifs of it, or how it should be done. Just hold me there with your hands and don't take your cock out when you cum. Do it as often as you want till it takes. I'll leave it for you to say. I won't ask for babies or tell you I'm not ready. Shoot it in me when you think the time is due. You know my legs are always open for whatever you want from me. I won't make a fuss or complain—but no conversations, please, no pleading, no wondering about it all. Impregnate me like I'm an animal that can take it 'cause I am. When the time is ready, just shoot me up. One night you might find yourself wanting it, after the cigarette is put out. It might occur to you in half your mind, sideways, wanting to try it out and see. Then try it out on me, fill me up with your load. I won't protest.

I am indifferent to whatever you do to me, as long as it feels as good as it did those three times. I am indifferent to whether you turn me into a sow you lead around the house with a leash, or if you lash me nightly, or if you throw my body into the bed or out of it. If you want my cunt to take your cum, or to turn me into an animal who can take it, I'll learn astrology. I'll be the stupidest whore you ever met; forget everything to kiss the head of the little nothing you give me, if you want it. And if you don't want it, it's your cock's head I'll kiss when you shove it up against my lips. I don't mind. You sleep and I'll tirelessly not sleep if that's the way your cock decides it should be. Whatever your cock decides.

You told me after he told you that he had made out with me, you said to Alexei, *You should try fucking her.* Lend me to Alexei then, to whichever one of your friends. I will fuck them like I'm fucking you, and think of you all the while—your body, and the greatness of you, that makes me do such things—and I will lick it up, whatever trails you leave and wherever you leave them. You call me. I'll be there with my whole mop of hair to clean it up.

Now all the windows in the kitchen are shining with the light from outside—where you are, Israel—while I am inside, on the phone, so you can see me with three guys tonight while you smoke on the chair you put into the corner of the room, only to leave it to lean down and look at what is going on between my legs. Blow your smoke up my cunt so I can taste it with my dizzy little puss—dizzy for you. Whatever you want me to do, I will do it, and whatever I don't want to do, I will do that too, and will want to.

Today the light came through the windows so beautifully that I didn't know if it was moonlight or sunlight I was seeing. I just stood there washing the dishes and breaking them on my wrists and hands like the long-suffering wife of a great poet, which you are not.

Now you want to go from me into the happy solitude of your maleness, with your need of no comfort from any woman. As you said, "I have finally learned not to need any woman."

Let my breasts not satisfy you then. Let my cunt bore you completely, so that even all the other cunts in the world can't distract you from the boredom that comes over you when you think of mine.

ACT
3

chapter 1

TWO SPIDERS

Margaux appeared at my door late one morning, knocking hard. I got up, weary, and went to answer it. She said, "You can't just not email me back after I sent you an email like that!"

"I thought you would never want to see me again," I told her.

"Just because I was upset doesn't mean it's all over!"

It had been several weeks since we had been in the same room together, and I wasn't sure we ever would be again. She followed me inside and watched me as I dressed. I wanted to explain myself, but there was nothing I could say. I never thought that my buying the dress would upset her. Also, I knew that if I said a single word, I would burst into tears, as I always did, always had, my entire life, whenever anything difficult had to be discussed. It always was too scary; a threat I had felt since childhood that at any moment a relationship might disappear with a poof because of something little I had done or said.

There in my crummy apartment, I felt like we were together after the Fall, expelled from a perfect garden. I always imagined a golden age—a time before the Fall, between me and every other person—before they knew my ugliness. Then I felt irrevocably uneasy once it had been revealed, when there could be no more appealing to their total trust and admiration, to that early, easy innocence.

But with Margaux sitting in my living room, a shiver of hope danced in my heart that she might forgive me for buying the dress. Why else had she come? I sat across from her on the small green sofa and was quiet for a few minutes. Then I asked her, trying not to let my tears fall, what the big problem had been with me buying the same dress she had bought. She looked out the window, sighed heavily, thought for a bit, then spoke.

"You know that hotel we stayed at in Miami?"

"Sure."

She asked if I remembered how our first night there, I noticed a spider on the bathroom wall. I had forgotten, but now I vaguely recalled.

"Well, you went to the bathroom, and you saw this daddy longlegs there. And I was like, *Do you want me to throw it out the window?* But you said, *No, let's keep it. Spiders are good.* I would have thrown it out, but you said let's not, so we agreed that we just didn't want it to wind up in our bed. We would keep our bathroom door closed the entire time. That way, the spider would stay in the bathroom and not crawl into our bed, which would be really disgusting.

"Anyway," she went on, "pretty soon you started to like it. You developed feelings for it. Like, whenever you went to the bathroom, you would look for it, and when you spotted it you'd speak to it. Sometimes it was in the tub, sometimes it was on the ceiling, sometimes it was sitting on the shower curtain. Then, after leaving the bathroom, you would say good-bye and close the door. You ended up becoming pretty affectionate with it."

"It became like a pet," I offered. "I remember that."

"Not something you could control, but something you could love. But if it had left the bathroom and invaded the bedroom, you probably wouldn't have liked it so much. But keeping it in the bathroom allowed you to love it. Keeping it in there was a sign that you loved it."

"Right."

"Then, on our last night there, we forgot to close the bathroom door—we were so drunk—and in the morning you woke up and it was beside your leg, and without even thinking, you smashed it under your hand."

"I remember," I said, uneasy.

"Well, that's like you buying the same dress as me. I'm doing a lot, what with letting you tape me, but—boundaries, Sheila. Barriers. We need them. They let you love someone. Otherwise you might kill them."

chapter 2

THEY WANDER THE CITY
ON DRUGS

The world is made up of poets and retards, and everyone's a poet, and everyone's a retard. I made a slip of the tongue the other day, and instead of saying I wanted an audience, said I wanted a Godience.

A man ran into a bar and began smashing all the beer mugs, throwing them to the floor. The bartender tried to stop him, and so did all the people drinking in the bar, but he was too violent. There was too much rage within him, and it overpowered all the others, who were fearful and afraid. At last, in his exhaustion, the man fell into a chair.

The man said, *Stop.* He got up and, stumbling, said to himself in a mumbling undertone, *Stop stop stop.* The people stood tense around him in a circle. He paused where he was, wavered a bit, then looked up at the dark, wooden, low-hanging ceiling. If he had reached up, he could have touched it. The police had already been called. Would they arrive too soon, before he had a chance to speak? He lifted his head. *I want to make an announcement,* he said. *I have an announcement to make. The man who loves God loves liberty. And as for the rest . . . license is what they love.*

Milton! That's who he had been reading that morning, or the morning before, or before he went on his bender. Now the policemen came to the door, and he was handed into their arms. In the corner, a blond-haired girl was crying, she had been so afraid. She was being comforted by a man. A policeman spoke. "Does anyone here know Milton? Has anyone here read Milton?"

Ryan said, "I read an introduction to one of his books. I only read the introductions. That's where all the information is, and that is where it all happens."

I was feeling nauseous. The whole commotion had made me practically sick, and this was a place reputed to refill the beer steins in the back with what was left behind in the pitchers and the glasses.

Ryan and I had enrolled in a clown class together. I was really excited about it. Since all the best artists know where the funny is, I thought if I went to clown school, I might know it too.

There were three former clowns leading the class because enrollment was so high. They had to hire two extra teachers so we would all get some individual attention. Ryan sat before me with his face painted white—I had painted it—and I was making his lips red. The other students were already way ahead of us. They had already moved on to the second person, so that half of them had their faces complete, while the others were being powdered. I hadn't even started on Ryan's cheeks, and both of us were growing concerned. I saw him nervously pulling at the paper towel I had tucked into the white collar of his T-shirt.

"I remember being told in kindergarten not to talk too much," I told him. "My teacher called me a chatterbox."

"Wow," Ryan said. "I don't have any traumatic stories like that."

I was saying how life is like a bar brawl and there is a cowboy shooting at your feet. It was me, Ryan, and a red-haired girl from class. We were walking through the dirty snow—snow gone bad from three months of pissing dogs and cars. In that moment, I felt as though I had made a mistake in comprehending everything. What would our punishment—for conceiving of things wrong—*be*? Life is not like dancing while a cowboy shoots at your feet!

"Guys!" I said. "Life is not like dancing in a bar brawl while a cowboy shoots at your feet!"

Then I woke the next morning, thankful I wasn't high.

I will give up pot because it makes me paranoid. But I will stay close to God because he makes me paranoid.

Margaux and I broke from our feelings of austerity with drugs. A good night of drinking and smoking, or a night of doing coke, and the next day, far from being hungover, our brains felt stilled and refreshed. It was like our insides had been set back to 00:00:00.

Margaux made the best paintings of her career the morning after we had been drinking for eight hours straight. She woke at nine and got up, and without thinking or hesitation went straight into her studio and began making paintings. I woke and cleaned the entire apartment, washed all the walls by hand. We didn't feel the need to call each other that day, and normally Margaux and I talked minimum once, for reassurance.

Soon it came to be that several times a week we would meet at Lot 16, just for a beer; then, not wanting to stop, we'd call someone for some coke; then it would be every night we wanted to relax like that after having worked all day—and the next day we'd wake and work better than if we hadn't got fucked up the night before. All that time we were calmly getting shitfaced, calmly waking at 00:00:00, and not calling each other until night fell, when we would ask like it was the first time ever if the other wanted to take a break. *Yes*. In the daytime, austerity. In the nighttime, oblivion. Daytime, nighttime. Daytime, nighttime. It went on and on like that, like throwing a ball from one hand to the other.

. . .

At one point Ryan tried to talk to us. "No one wants to be friends with you two, and when they see you, they avoid you. Sheila, you never come to clown class anymore."

"Who gives a fuck about clown class," I said, giving a kick to the sidewalk with my foot.

We were following our instincts, same as we had always done.

I wanted to take a big pipe and swing it against someone's throat. I wanted to see their body buckle back and red shoot from their throat like a burst water main. Psychoanalytic drugs.

Though it was cold, we'd pace through the city at night. Now in one direction, now another. Always changing direction. *Should we go down this alley? Fine. Do you want to go up this alley? Yes, let's do it. But we just came down this alley. That's okay, we'll go up it again.* We went up it and down it, up it and down. *If we keep walking through this alley, we'll tread a rut into it. That's okay, I prefer pacing to getting somewhere.* Up it and down, up and down. Then in the mornings Margaux would paint, and I would wash the walls.

It was getting colder. We told ourselves that these were the happiest days of our lives. Never had I had a routine. Never had Margaux had a system that worked so well. In the mornings there was frost on the windows. I went to the salon. There was beauty everywhere.

. . .

The lecture portion of class was held in a university class-
room with coliseum-style seating. Everyone sat in the dark
in their boots, having trekked in the snow with them, so
that by the end of the lecture we all had puddles of slush
beneath our feet. Pulling on our heavy coats at the end of
class, we tried not to trail the hems of our sleeves in the
little puddle of snow and muck. I sat with my coat on and
could hardly see the page, the lights were dimmed so low.
Before us on the screen was projected a slide of a man on a
mountaintop by Caspar David Friedrich. The professor's
voice was amplified with her mike. "In the nineteenth
century—"

The nineteenth century, I thought, snickering.

"—artists were compelled by the idea of the sublime,
which was the most elevated expression of the harmony
between nature and man. By contemplating nature, a figure like this one on the mountaintop would be inspired with
reverence for the majesty of what God created—both hum-
bled by it and also elevated by it because he, as a witness
and an observer, had a privileged relation to all of creation—
both of it and standing outside it to contemplate it. It was
through contemplating nature that one would gain this
experience of the sublime, so you tend to find in pictures
from this time—"

Slide changed.

"—this theme repeated: the untamed and overwhelming
power and beauty of nature, and the witness to it, somewhere

in the painting, a stand-in for the viewer and the painter. Without a witness to the scene—"

Right! Right! It is not a picture of the sublime! Suddenly I understood our walks, mine and Margaux's, through the alleys, up them and down them on our drugs.

"There is no sublime in it," Margaux told me.

Now she was getting more interested in painting in the nights as well, and when I would call to see if she wanted to take a break from painting and go with me to drink, she would say no. She even told me, the one night she did come out, that she only had an hour. When I tried to explain what I had learned in class about the sublime, she didn't think it had anything to do with us or why we liked our drugs.

"We like our drugs for the opposite feeling," she said, "for the feeling of nullity. Not for the awesome power of the universe."

"No! No! We ingest it. We swallow it, we put it inside us—the awesome power of the universe. We're not looking at a mountain range because there are no mountain ranges in the city."

"That doesn't mean we're trying to put the mountain range inside us—so that we can feel the power of witnessing a mountain range, as in a Caspar David Friedrich painting."

"That's exactly what it is," I said, looking her in the face.

Margaux shook her head. I nodded mine.

"I can see it," I said. She shook her head.

We could see no trees and we could see no mountains from where we lived. When we looked out the window we saw cars, we saw people, we saw traffic lights and buildings just like ours. Sometimes the past came to greet us, and there were two policemen sitting atop their horses, walking down the side street I was living on, and I woke to the sounds of the horses in the road. I raised myself in bed and looked out the window. When a car came by, the policemen pulled on the horses' reins and the horses stopped, and the policemen and the horses waited patiently for the car to go by, one horse shaking its tail in the road.

I liked lying there in the dead of night, watching the snow swirl beneath the streetlights. It looked to me like the harmony between nature and man, that we should build such streetlights and nature deliver such blustery snow.

I didn't envy the teenage girls in their tight jeans with the curve of their round asses showing beneath their puffy jackets. They walked through the snow with their girl-friends who dressed alike, their hair hanging below their shoulders, shopping bags in hand. I regarded them like deer or any natural phenomena—not designed specifically to please me, but pleasing all the same.

In the dead of night I would lie awake, gazing at the ceiling, and, thinking I heard the sound of horses, I would turn my body to look out the window, but I only saw the horses that once and never again.

I remembered the man who came into the bar, crashing the glasses against the floor. *Liberty is freedom, and license is freedom at the expense of God. Man can do nothing directly to achieve his own freedom. What he can do is to indicate his willingness to be set free by knocking down his idols, so allow the Word of God to circulate freely in human society.* I wanted to discuss this with Ryan some more, but when I went to his place and knocked on his door, he was not there. I decided to go to the Communist's Daughter and sit at the small bar. My gut suggested that the man who was breaking bottles was the hero. I sensed something immovable in the center of him—maybe not admirable, but strong and stable and straight.

I knew as I walked that the planet was spinning at a very high speed, but that this did not prevent everything from staying in its place, and everything from seeming solid and straight. If the earth did not spin on its axis, this would not be the case. I might have been wrong, but as I had nobody to discuss it with, I was not contradicted in my thinking. When I arrived at the bar, I was pleased but not surprised to see Ryan sitting there. It was the place he most liked to drink at, and he was doing it again. He moved aside, and I sat down next to him. I asked him how important he thought it was for the earth to spin on its axis, and he said, "I don't really know."

The bartender, who was wiping down a spill, overheard

this and remarked, "Of all of my customers, the two of you seem to know the least about science."

"Are other people always talking about science?" I asked.

"Often," he said and, hooking the rag back over the hook, he said it again. "Often."

I wanted so much to make a retort that would redeem us both, but I could think of nothing before he was off filling up a half pint of beer for someone else—another customer, who knew more about science than Ryan or I did.

"It doesn't matter," I said, turning to Ryan, but his face was clouded over.

He said, "If you think his opinion is going to shake me from my axis, you're wrong! My axis is solid and stable and straight, and I have always spun around it—*always*—not around his opinion or yours!"

Night fell, but then, there are always holes to fall into.

I don't want 00:00:00 anymore. It is banal. Yet in the pitch-perfect moments of life, I say to myself that I have followed my rules wisely, and that the surge of sublimity that flows within me is the gods' reward.

Now when I wake in the mornings, I look out the window in the hopes that a policeman on a horse will pass by. When it doesn't happen, I untangle myself from the sheets and get up and go to the mirror to start my day. I produce a haughty, superior expression to intimidate myself into thinking I'm cool, cooler than I am. I make my eyes as world-weary as possible, like a fashion model's, then I think, *You're a charlatan. You love everything you were ever given.*

I want more than to appear sufficiently cool in my own eyes—though this would be admitting that all my vanity and primping has been a waste. Every glance into the mirror and the expressions I've contrived to intimidate myself—fatuous. It is perhaps better to continue along the path toward beauty I have started on, and to hope that, if I am rigorous enough in following this path, it will lead me somewhere great. Then, if I do succeed in turning myself into an idol, it will not have been for nothing.

I am not thinking of the one who said that in order to gain life, you have to lose it. If I lose it, I will be like the earth spinning off its axis into infinity, and who knows, without being something I can gaze at and admire, if I will ever find my way back.

But I can only imagine what would happen to all the stuff of the earth if the earth was to spin off its axis. I think trees would crash into cars, but I don't know enough science to say.

chapter 3

ANTHONY AND URI

The next several weeks I worked double shifts at the salon, to distract myself from the nothing that made up my days. One afternoon, Sholem came in to have his hair washed. He said he was still feeling dirty from making his ugly painting, and he wanted to wash away that feeling. It often happened that people came to the salon for that very reason—more than anyone would guess. Seating him at a basin, I put a towel around his neck and guided his head back into the bowl, then turned on the water and adjusted the temperature on my hand. Uri had recently started me on shampooing. I put the spray near the crown of his head, and as the water flowed down, I asked, "Is it too hot? Too cold?"

"Just right."

When it came time for the conditioner, I gave him a head massage, the way I had been taught, but he was tense, his shoulders straining toward his neck, and his neck was very rigid. Then he blurted out, "Oh, why did Margaux make us *do* this?"

SHEILA

Do what? The Ugly Painting Competition?

SHOLEM

Yes, the Ugly Painting Competition! I've been thinking about it a lot, you know, because I still can't understand why she'd want me to have these bad feelings, and the only thing I can come up with is that she must be going through a painting crisis. She wants to make the worst possible paintings out of some mistrust of painting.

SHEILA

A painting crisis! But she never stops painting! She's painting all the time.

SHOLEM

But she hasn't begun her ugly painting yet, has she? And why not? When you ask her, she just shrugs it off. But it's been *months*! I saw her at an opening last night, and she just kept saying that paintings don't matter. I find it really depressing, and it makes no sense. It's so frustrating!

SHEILA

But she's always spoken like that.

SHOLEM

But don't you think it's strange? And the strangest thing about her crisis is that it's late.

SHEILA

It's what? *Late?*

SHOLEM

Late! Most painters go through their crisis in art school, because that's where you're surrounded by all these people telling you that, you know, painting is dead. So I can't understand why she's going through this crisis *now*, when everyone loves her work, when the critics do, and when she has a dealer who's a consummate believer in painting. Why *now*? And I think it's because Margaux doesn't trust paint-ing. She doesn't trust it to be a powerful communicator, so she has to make the worst painting possible. Then, if there's still some beauty or value at the end, it will restore her faith in painting.

I led Sholem to an empty station and swiveled the chair around. He sat, and I turned him to face the mirror. I took the comb from my apron and dipped it in the Barbicide, so he could see for himself—whether he was consciously worried or not—that it was free of germs, and I flung off the excess liquid and drew it through his hair, looking down at his head. Ruby came up and put her hand on my arm.

"Use the mirror," she told me. "The mirror is a tool."

I nodded. I looked at Sholem's head in the mirror. He seemed glum. I went to get some cream to settle his Jewish curls, then ran my hands through his hair.

SHOLEM

Of course, it's a brilliant plan, because there's no *way* Margaux can make an ugly painting. She just *can't*! How is she going to reverse her color sense? How is she going to reverse her amazing compositional sense, her brushstroke, her line? I have to say that if Margaux brings something to the competition that she's embarrassed about, a painting that she is really, truly ashamed of, or one that is actually bad—I will be *agog*.

I went to get one of the stylists, because I was not experienced enough to blow-dry. But before I left, I asked Sholem if he felt any cleaner than he had felt before. He shook his head simply. "No. For some reason I only feel worse."

Then he said, "Listen—everything I said about Margaux is just between you, me, and the walls. Don't tell her I said any of this."

"Okay," I said, for I wanted him to like and trust me.

That afternoon, walking back and forth through the salon, picking up towels and sweeping the floor, I kept my attention on Anthony—one of the dozen stylists who worked there. Uri did everything so beautifully, but I couldn't say I loved him. I admired and respected him, but I had genuine love for Anthony. Maybe because I felt he was like me, I saw him with my heart, not my mind. He worked at a station in the corner of the salon and had been working there for nine years. A few weeks ago, I began overhearing gossip: *Why doesn't Uri fire Anthony? Anthony is so immature and arrogant! He made Leslie cry!* Anthony was always boasting about how he had cut hair in Los Angeles, Miami, and New York, and had been asked to teach in various salons. He was better than this city. If he hadn't met his wife, he would be in one of those cities right now. Did we know that he had once colored Lindsay Lohan's hair? He claimed that nobody in the world cut the way he did, a method he called *fluid motion cutting*, whereby he'd move quickly around a client's head. To watch him was like watching an athletic performance. He would dye customers' hair without telling them, if he thought it would make them look better, and though some gazed into the mirror with tears of regret, no one protested, for they felt they were dealing with an artist.

And that was how Anthony saw himself—as an artist—whereas Uri had the simple goal of the craftsman: excellence. He was so dedicated to the business that he almost died three years ago from blood leaking into his brain. He did everything perfectly, and the same way every time—but he was not without some cruelty, I was beginning to see, which made his customers reliant on him, because he knew their flaws. He was the first to tell them that they had gray hair, even before they saw it. Or he'd explain that their hairline was receding, or thinning at the back. But he was consistent, and it was hard to find fault. With Anthony, you never knew what you were getting. He was a new man every day.

I once mentioned Anthony's accomplishments to Uri, and Uri laughed robustly. "Oh yes, the amazing Anthony! Tell me then, if he's so amazing, why doesn't he have his own shop?" This was Anthony's greatest regret, though he hid his shame. The more Uri took me under his wing, the more Anthony tried to win my confidence, cornering me in the back room and telling me about his life; how he had almost opened a salon five years back, but then the seller took it off the market—he did not know why—and a month later the economy collapsed, and then it was impossible. He ran a consulting business on the side—this salon was not his whole world!—but when I asked if I could have one of his business cards, he made a big show of being affronted. He never gave out business cards! That would be tacky.

Just before closing that day, Anthony's children were paraded in—three sweet toddlers—and Anthony had me wash their silky, childish hair. Seeing me doing this, Uri came up and put his hand on my shoulder and said in a booming voice, "Some hairdressers think they are gods because you have people all the time telling you how incredible you are. But a good hairdresser does not think he's a god!"

I didn't want to write this on my arm.

When I was finished, I hung up my rubber apron in the

back room and changed from my low heels into winter boots and headed straight for Israel's.

Sheila's mother prays that Sheila will help her . . .

1. I am renting a dumpster and throwing out all the garbage from the basement and the garage. Hopefully this weekend or at most in two weeks.

2. I do not want to throw out my daughter's things; she has lots of wonderful things here, pictures and more.

3. May she come over one day and sort out what is garbage. I do not want to throw it all out, but I am tempted.

4. I know it is a bad time for my daughter. But it's been a bad time for her ever since she moved out. She will never ever have the time for it, and I do understand. It is a very low priority. But it is not a low priority for me.

5. I have been living here for almost thirty years, and I don't want to go on with my reasoning, I am just ready to do it! Please make her come over now, not when she has the time for it, for she will never have the time for it.

6. Once I rent the dumpster, I might as well throw out what belongs to my daughter. Ninety-nine percent of the stuff is just garbage. That is probably why she doesn't do it. Why would she spend her time with garbage?

7. I don't want to be the storage place for garbage anymore. It is a huge clutter on my brain! Perhaps I can figure out something better for my basement. I just want it free of the piles of garbage. Starting with my ex-husband's pinball machine.

8. Please let her come over and be nice to me and do it. If I do end up throwing out her things, neither of us will ever forgive me.

9. If my daughter comes over, she will make me very happy.

1. Yesterday, at a barbecue, somebody asked me if I had any kids. I almost said, *I used to have kids.* I don't think it's all my fault that I said that.

· *chapter 4* ·

SHEILA BEGINS AGAIN

Sheila sits with Misha in a cheap Italian restaurant, late at night, in the back, under the fluorescent lights. There are people at every table.

SHEILA

(*to the waiter*) I want the "whole grilled rainbow."

Misha nods at the waiter; the waiter leaves.

SHEILA

I don't know if that was the right choice but?

MISHA

It's all right.

SHEILA

(*hyped up*) I'm finding it so confusing with him! And I'm really aware in this situation, like, *Oh, we're not going to get married*, you know? It doesn't have that big dream attached. Even though I don't think of myself as somebody with that big dream, obviously I am, because I have been—

MISHA

—married, yeah. I guess when I was single and promiscuous, a lot of what I kind of objected to was the idea that those two things had to go together.

SHEILA

But how can you *not* have an emotional relationship?

MISHA

You *do* have an emotional relationship, but it's just a different kind. Like, it's really *fun* to have sex with people. You spend a lot of time in your life going out and having coffee with people you're not friends with. You don't want them to call you at two in the morning if they're feeling down, you're not going to help them move house, they're not dear friends. But you do understand that *Oh, it's thrilling to have*—

SHEILA

—this exchange?

MISHA

Yeah! And on the whole it makes you an intellectually more interesting person. The same might be true of sex. It seems very analogous. Like, *Oh, it's really fun to have sex with different people.* Even if you liked to play squash, and you wanted to play squash with different people—

SHEILA

But sex is different from *squash*, no?

Misha shrugs.

I spent the next few days at Israel's with my cell phone battery dead, working on my blow jobs, really trying to make them something perfect. I started feeling proud, like I was doing something useful in the world—and not for one moment did I think to myself that I should be doing something more old-fashionedly important, like finishing a play.

When I arrived home late one night, I found a yellow envelope in my mailbox. I took it to my room and opened it, and the gray dust from inside went all over my hands and face. Inside the envelope was my tape recorder. I hadn't seen it in so long! I didn't even realize it was gone. I turned it on, and a light flashed—one new file—noting a day I had not recorded; a day I had been at Israel's.

Margaux's voice comes out softly . . .

1. It's me. I'm not sure where the recording part is. I'm sitting in our studio, but I'm at your desk. I never noticed before that it's completely chalk-blue.
2. It seems like such a strange desk, now that you're gone.
3. I came into the studio tonight and there's an art opening downstairs, so they gave me a glass of wine. So now I'm just looking at the glass of wine. But it feels very different than when you're here.
4. My rule is that I'm not allowed to erase anything that I record . . . I tell myself after something I would have erased.
5. The sky is so beautiful today, right now, out the window.

1. Last night, Misha and I were looking at the MacArthur Fellowship website. But I think you have to live in the U.S. to get them. And I think you have to be a genius.
2. It was funny. I had no feelings of insecurity looking at the MacArthur Fellowships, or at all the people who won them. I felt so happy looking at it.
3. It felt so much nicer than an art magazine or other types of reward systems. I guess it's a grant for potential. But it was so nice to think that there are these quiet people doing these wonderful things, and that someone tries to notice that. It maybe felt like a more

beautiful illustration of ambition. Or a better kind of
ambition. Like not to be a genius, and not to be . . .

4. Just to do good work . . . to have potential . . . to be
   recognized in your field among other people, as
   though you're progressing somewhere collectively,
   rather than competing.

1. I think I do better with the recordings when you're
   here. I think what I want to do right now is just
   record this, then go over to my desk and work. And
   so to pretend like you're here.
2. The quieter I am in your tape recorder, the more it
   feels like you're here.

1. (*sighs*) I always had a fantasy of meeting a girl . . . who
   was as serious as I was.

I wasn't sure if this delivery was Margaux's way of telling
me to get to work on my play—or that she missed me in
the studio, or even that there was money for geniuses—but
somehow it all felt possible. It suddenly felt like the simplest
thing. Why had I forgotten all the ways that it was natural
and easy for me to work?

A feeling of my true freedom came up inside me, and I
sat down before my computer and calmly transcribed the
message Margaux had left me on the tape recorder. Then I
wrote up the narrative of what happened to us in Miami,
putting down all the things we said; the private sentiments

that only I knew. I wrote fluidly for three or four hours. And I felt so happy doing it, so at home. There was a peace and security in me. It wasn't my play, but it felt good—far better than fiddling with the dialogue of Ms. Oddi and Mrs. Sing, as I had been doing for so long. I felt closer to knowing something about reality, closer to some truth.

Printing it out and reading it over, a feeling of pride bloomed in me like spring, like something new was being born.

· *chapter 5* ·

THE WHITE MEN GO TO AFRICA

Sheila invites to dinner one of the former directors of her play, Ben, and his playwright collaborator, Andrew. Margaux is there, too. Sheila wants to see what Ben has been doing since they worked on her play and wants to hear about the play he's directing now. She is curious to see where theater's at, compared with where it was at ten months ago. The dinner is nearing its end. The table is littered with the remains of bread and cheese and meat and peas. Sheila's silver tape recorder and Ben's sil-ver tape recorder lie opposite each other amid the plates of food like two silver guns.

BEN

Talk is cheap, you know.

SHEILA

Talk is cheap?

MARGAUX

Talk is cheap—so you went to Africa.

BEN

Yup.

MARGAUX

'Cause Africa's not cheap.

BEN

Actually, Africa's pretty cheap.

MARGAUX

Where in Africa did you go?

ANDREW

Johannesburg. Johannesburg and Cape Town.

BEN

We had slightly different reasons for going, I think, but they found some mutual expression in the idea of going to Africa. For me, it was because my life in theater is so consuming and busy and it's such a kind of insular world in a lot of ways, and I was dissatisfied with the absence of doing meaningful—what I felt was meaningful—I didn't feel I was spending my time in the most meaningful way possible, and I wanted to bring a more meaningful, uh, component to the work I was doing.

SHEILA

In a more activist kind of way?

BEN

Potentially. I got fed up with my own narcissism basically. I just felt like I was being narcissistic. And it was becoming really difficult to separate my desire to create art from my narcissism. Of course, I felt incredibly silly about going to Africa. It felt like a really stupid thing to do. You go there— what are you going to do?

ANDREW

It's also very fashionable.

BEN

It's *very* fashionable, you know.

ANDREW

And it's so easily a continuation of the narcissism.

SHEILA

That's what I was going to say.

BEN

But what really impressed me about being there was just talking to these people, and seeing all the millions of ways that you could—with so little effort—expand your world and be helpful and involved. And it was really easy to see in a place like Africa 'cause things are so extreme. It was just such a crushing awakening of the colossal injustice of the way our world works economically, whereas here—

ANDREW

It's disguised.

BEN

It's disguised. It's so easy to forget.

MARGAUX

Seems kind of hard to forget; I don't know.

BEN

Does it?

MARGAUX

Yeah, it really does.

BEN

Not to me. And there—well, the most profound experience I had was, like, meeting people who live in extreme poverty or whatever, and I started to realize the extent to which I objectify poor people, and the ways we objectify poverty in order to tolerate the incredible disparity and lack of justice in the world—and what I experienced there was like, *Oh my God! These are all people! These are a million people that live in shacks that are awesome people, that are smart and, you know, are people.*

ANDREW

Yeah—or not even smart—are just people.

BEN

We visited this one woman who was living in this real little shithole. Do you remember which one I'm talking about?

ANDREW

Yeah.

BEN

How many kids did she have?

ANDREW

Three.

BEN

I think four. And several of them had HIV. And she had HIV obviously. And her husband had, I don't know, died last month from AIDS. She had just gotten a new boyfriend, and she has this new little baby who probably has AIDS, and the boyfriend is clearly going to get AIDS—I don't know . . .

ANDREW

Just the scale of dependency of women upon men there was shocking. Just to see what it actually means for women to be dependent on men was *shocking*. And how the men have totally failed—

BEN

—and how women are doing everything. *Everything!*

SHEILA

What do you mean the women are doing everything and the men aren't doing anything?

BEN

The women are doing *everything*—they're raising the kids, they're bringing in the money for the kids, they're the ones who are—

ANDREW

—organizing communities.

BEN

Organizing all the movements. They're doing *everything*!

SHEILA

And what are the men doing?

BEN

Drinking.

ANDREW

Drinking and hanging out.

BEN

Just wallowing and lost. Lost.

Ben gets up and starts pacing around the table.

You step for one minute outside of your privilege, your stresses and concerns, and you see something that's worth responding to. But then you come back, and it's a couple months later, and it's like, *What was that?* You're inundated with—or I am, anyways—like there's no room in my life for *anything.* I can barely keep up the standard of living I need. The idea of adding to that a concern for others and making time for others is *really* daunting. But at the same time I've been feeling right now—really acutely—the injustice of the circumstances some people are born into versus others, and I would like to be able to address that because, you know, the world is tremendously unfair, and it shouldn't be that unfair for the vast majority of people.

MARGAUX

I'm reading *Sirens of Titan*—the Kurt Vonnegut?—where it's the culture of unfairness? So after the revolution people have bags of weights on them to make it balanced for people that have good luck, or people that are—yeah, good luck, so that covers everything—class, race, gender . . .

BEN

Sure, sure.

MARGAUX

And really beautiful women smear their faces with really disgusting makeup to—and sort of have a hunch.

No one says anything.

BEN

To me, the deeper place is like, I've always wanted to be a theater artist, and I've succeeded to the extent to which I—to which my dreams allow. But so what, you know? I'm not convinced that this is a good use of one's time. There are so many other things one could be doing with one's life. It's a very particular kind of experience, being a theater director. Nervous-system-wise, it's a very particular kind of activity. It's a very narcissistic activity.

MARGAUX

(*loudly*) You guys keep saying *narcissism*; what do you mean by that exactly?

BEN

I mean that one is very involved in one's own mind.

SHEILA

But *all* art is like that. Books and paintings and—

BEN

Sure, sure.

MARGAUX

Even activism is very involved with righteousness, you know.

Long pause.

SHEILA

So where are you guys with your collaboration? Is your play going to talk about this?

BEN

Uh . . . maybe. I hope so. In some kind of way. A simple way to talk about it is that it's about us, and about our embarking on a project together, and we're trying to make something together as friends, trying to take each other out of ourselves and into the world, and it evolves into an actual engagement in the world. Then comes the discovery of something that we're interested in replacing ourselves with.

ANDREW

We're working with an actress. She's doing a lot of the voices of the women we spoke to there, so suddenly in the middle of the play, Ben and I will kind of leave the stage so she can talk . . .

BEN

Ultimately what we'd like to do is tell somebody else's story (*laughs a bit*)—to build a bridge from our story to another story that we think is important to tell, then tell that story somehow. So we're acting in the play right now, and our little challenge to ourselves is that maybe we'll get off the stage at some point.

Sheila stands up.

SHEILA

Should I bring out the dessert?

MARGAUX

(*rising*) Oh, I can bring it out.

BEN

You know, making art but not boring people . . .

SHEILA

Really? That's amusing. I like boring people. I think it's a
virtue. People *should* be a little bored.

MARGAUX

(*exiting*) Girls aren't as good at being boring.

SHEILA

(*exiting*) Girls aren't as good at being boring?

MARGAUX

Maybe.

All the white men I know are going to Africa. They want
to tell the stories of African women. They are so serious.
They lectured me about my lack of morality. *Sure*, I said.
Sure, if they would like to present themselves as role mod-
els for teenage girls, what have I got on them? Only a natu-

ral empathy that no one could guess at from the way I have been living. They come at life from the outside, those white boys who went to Africa. To have to wear on the outside one's curiosity, one's pity, one's guilt . . .

All I want is to look back with no regrets. And perhaps go to Africa and return with the story of an impoverished black woman whose boyfriend has AIDS and drinks, and whose four babies have AIDS and drink—to communicate something of greater importance to North Americans than the poverty of my soul.

Later that evening, Sheila and Margaux wipe their hands on a towel, having cleaned up after dinner. They go onto the front steps and sit facing the street. A halo of light emanates from a street lamp across the road; a fuzzy, translucent white crystal of light against the dark blue sky, sort of like descriptions of the artist Robert Irwin's luminescent disks, which people once went rapturous about, calling them moon-silver, incandescent, ethereal, dropped from heaven.

SHEILA

How can these artists we read about—who have been married five or six times—how can they have enough time for all that life, *and* also make art?

MARGAUX

And have a heroin addiction?

SHEILA

Either there's something I'm not understanding, or that was another point in history.

MARGAUX

You know, visually, I think I always understood that looking at a Pollock painting or looking at a brick wall—like, the brick wall might be more interesting for me. But because the brick wall might be more interesting for me, I never quite understood why it was important to make things sometimes.

SHEILA

(*excited*) I made something!

MARGAUX

What?

SHEILA

I'll tell you . . .

Sheila reaches behind her back, then grows scared and changes her mind.

You know, the other day, Sholem came into the salon—

MARGAUX

I saw him in the street yesterday, buying new clothes.

SHEILA

He feels dirty because of the ugly painting he made!

Then I told her about how Sholem had gone about making his ugly painting—making a list of all the things he found ugly, and putting them in a painting.

Margaux shakes her head.

MARGAUX

That's what I was afraid of. Sholem should have been ugly with all of his heart—from his center, not from a list!

SHEILA

I know! He also told me he thinks you're in the middle of a painting crisis.

MARGAUX

What! He *said* that? Oh my God, I'm so totally *not* having a painting crisis! Just 'cause I don't automatically have respect for paintings. But Sholem *does.* He's so reverent: *Oh, it's a painting!* Well, so *what?* Frankly, I'm surprised by his total interest in it.

SHEILA

But that's natural, isn't it, for someone who's a painter to be interested in paintings?

MARGAUX

I'm interested in *meaning,* not paintings. Paintings can be pretty meaningless, you know. Like, it's insane! I want to create complete meaning in art that's even better than political meaning! And Sholem wants to make the most flawless paintings in the world. And you—you want to be the human ideal! We're crazy. We all want such big things!

What was so crazy about wanting to be the human ideal? That upset me.

SHEILA

Have you made your ugly painting yet?

MARGAUX

Not yet.

SHEILA

Why not?

MARGAUX

I don't know! *Ugly, beautiful*—I don't even understand what those words mean.

SHEILA

Then why did you agree to the competition?

MARGAUX

I'm doing it for *him*! I thought it would be interesting for Sholem, because when there's such resistance, as there was . . .

I didn't want to talk about Sholem anymore. I pulled some pages out from behind me, rolled up like a cylinder. "Take this," I said, pressing it into her hand. Margaux held it, turning it around.

"What is it?"

I suddenly grew excited. I explained about how the other night, after she had returned to me my tape recorder, I began writing about us in Miami, and transcribed our conversations from that trip. I wanted her to read it now.

"I don't want to see it!"

"Why?"

"I don't know!"

Her expression of aversion struck me. It recalled to me a warm afternoon as a teenager, when I had been hanging out with my high school boyfriend at his father's place. We were sitting on his father's couch. Suddenly and without warning, he unzipped his pants and pulled out his cock. I had burst into tears of shock—it was the first adult penis I had ever seen, and without ceremony or warning—and I left the apartment, furious. I wouldn't talk to him for two whole weeks. Then I came to love him.

"I want you to see it," I said, thrusting it in her direction, hurt. She reached out reluctantly, timidly, and took it. A feeling of satisfaction rose in my being, such that I couldn't imagine she would feel any way but as impressed by its power and beauty as I was.

chapter 6

THE ART SHOW

One week later, I went to see a group show that Paul Petro curated. My plan was to drop in for just ten minutes, then head home. When I arrived, a group of people were standing by the front doors, smoking. A girl I hardly knew turned to me with a friendly smile, and I grinned widely back.

Inside the white-walled space, Paul, a tall man with smooth skin and a deep tan, came up to me and smiled. He asked me if I had seen Margaux's painting yet. I said no, I had no idea she was in the show! We went to the back and he got me a beer, then I followed him up to the second floor. I went with him into the front room, and we stood there together, facing the largest painting Margaux had ever made. It was still wet. And it was terrible to behold.

She had depicted herself as a fat, chubby-cheeked Buddha figurine, with a smug, sly smile wiped across her face.

In the background were cotton balls. Her body was made of shiny porcelain, and jewels and rings crowded her fingers and arms. She sat cross-legged, her peroxide hair falling thinly over her shoulders, and her expression was one of greedy self-satisfaction. It was utterly grotesque. The title, printed on a small card, was *Margaux Souvenir.*

A cold wash ran through my body. Paul laughed, understanding nothing, but I knew how Margaux felt about the world. She saw no glory in being Buddha, and had never painted herself this way before. Buddha was the one who turned his back on the suffering of the world to sweeten himself with good feelings—privileged feelings of benevolence and purity, just like her worst fears about what it meant to be a painter.

I thanked Paul and turned and went slowly down the stairs, careful not to fall, my heart racing and feeling nauseated. Leaving my half-empty beer bottle on his desk, I made it out the front door and headed straight for Margaux's apartment, three blocks away.

chapter 7

MARGAUX QUILTS

I knocked on the front door of Misha and Margaux's, but no one answered. I used my key to get in, then went up to the second floor. The door to their place was open, and I went straight through the kitchen and into the bedroom, where I found Margaux in the dark, sitting upright on their bed, watching a movie and quilting. She glanced at me with the unblinking eyes of an animal, her face washed in blue. It had been a week since we had seen each other last.

"I was just at Paul Petro's. I saw your ugly painting there."

"Oh? You found it ugly?" She turned a cold, hard look at her quilt.

A loose, frightened feeling ran through my whole body, then my body grew heavy, as if weighed down with shit. I wanted to take back what I had written about us in those pages; whatever she had read to make her—us— seem so awful. But I could no more disown it than my teenage boyfriend could have wiped from my mind how he had portrayed me in his play. It happened. I thought of apologizing—but couldn't. Women apologize too much, I once decided, and made myself stop, and now found it incredibly difficult to tell anyone I was sorry.

Margaux said, "I once had a friend in art school, who I shared a studio with. She ran away to become a Buddhist and to live in a Buddhist colony in Colorado. She had been a painter, too, but when I went to visit her, she was just painting pretty colors on the insides of the temples that only the rich people who had reached the highest spiritual plane could see. I always thought that would never be me."

Her face fell while I stood there, stunned. For a long time I didn't say anything. I wanted to tell her that being a painter was *not* meaningless, decadent, narcissistic, and vain, but how could I know, for sure? All I knew, down to the deepest part of my being, was that if I lived the life that was truly inside me, near her, I would only cause her pain. I didn't have any faith that whatever I might say wouldn't hurt her doubly and only make things worse.

"I think I should go," I said.

She agreed.

I turned and left her apartment, hesitating, slowly, hoping she would call me back, but she did not. Making my way down the hall, I passed her studio and glanced inside. Through the half-closed door I saw no canvases, no brushes, no paint. I felt something drop inside of me, like gravity had shifted, like when you suddenly realize the person you have been staring at is missing a limb.

chapter 8

SHEILA QUAKES

Down in the street I got onto my bike and biked as fast as I could to one of the abandoned fields by the foot of the city, down near the water, spread out beneath the elevated highway. No one tended to the land there. No one developed it. It existed for no one, this dead-grass expanse.

I had come too close and hurt her—killed whatever in Margaux made art, whatever allowed her to tell herself that it was all right to be a painter in the face of all her doubts. I knew why and how it had happened. Instead of sitting down and writing my play with *my* words—using *my* imagination, pulling up the words from the solitude and privacy of my soul—I had used *her* words, stolen what was *hers*. I had plagiarized her being and mixed it up with the ugliness that was mine! Then she had looked into it and, like looking in a funhouse mirror, believed the decadent, narcissistic person she saw was *her*—when really it was *me*. Unwilling to be naked, I had made her naked instead. I had not worked hard or at all.

I had cheated.

Shame covered my face and hands. I would abandon my play for good. I would never tape us again! I climbed under the fence and ran down the hill and wandered off through the field in pain. The moon was out and full, and everything was shivering in the moon's silvery light. I thought about nature, and that I was in nature, and then I said to myself, *You* are *nature*. My eyes caught the edge of something in the sky—a beautiful sign perched over the highway that had been erected so long ago by a manufacturer of washers and dryers. Its bright white bulbs outlined in pink formed the magical word: *Inglis*. I stood there staring at it, wondering, near tears, if there could be, in heaven or on earth, anything more beautiful than this bright sign over this dead field, and how amazing it was what human nature—*Inglis*—and nature-nature—the field—could make in harmony with each other.

I must have been standing there like that for twenty minutes, when I noticed something: a sentence scrolling beneath it in bright LEDs. It had been scrolling the entire time I'd been there, but only just now did I see what it said: *MAKE THE DECISIONS THAT BENEFIT EVERYONE. MAKE THE DECISIONS THAT BENEFIT EVERYONE.*

My heart caught on my rib. If only I could figure out

what that was—the decision that would benefit everyone—I would do it!

Kneeling in the grass, Sheila's heart races her an email . . .

1. How terrible will be the day of judgment, Amen. How terrible will be the judgment when you walk down the street and catch yourself in a store window. And you will be judged.
2. Smash the tops of the pillars so that even the bottom of the doors will shake. Make the pillars fall on the people's heads; anyone left alive, I will kill with a sword.
3. Not one person will get away. No one will escape. If they dig down as deep as the place of the dead, I will pull them up. If they climb into heaven, I will bring them down. Forget your drugs, forget your sex, for you will be brought down if you are up, and you will be brought up if you are down in the place of the dead, to the middle place that is intended for you, Amen.
4. Do not hide at the top of Mount Carmel or at the bottom of the sea with the tropical fish and a heavy tank of oxygen on your back, for I will find you even there. And if you are happy, I will make you sad, and if you have been innocent, I will make you guilty. I will command a snake to bite you, and then you

will become like a snake to others, telling them all
your troubles and troubling their innocence!

5. I will keep watch to give them trouble, not do them
good.

6. Cry for the dead, for *Inglis* has no mercy on the dead.
Even in the heavens there is no looking forward to
or looking back from, just a pure white burning in
the light.

7. So walk up the hills and run down the hills, ascend
the stairs and descend them, sit and lie and dance and
stand, for there will be no moving in the land of
judgment. There will be no sitting or fidgeting or
smoking or sleeping. There will only be a burning
without your body in the light. I will destroy all you
have known, and all you will know is me.

8. Be like a shaking piece of grain in a sifter.

9. Shake like a little piece of grain upon a sieve.

10. Rattle and stir like a little piece of soil in a sifter.

11. Not even the tiniest stone falls through.

I would go to where she couldn't see me, or be pained by
me anymore—where no one would know what I had done.
Like a good spider—locked safely away—I would leave the
city to her.

Then maybe one day, in the future, with the bad feelings I had caused in her erased from her heart, and all
memory of the Miami piece and our travels and me forgotten, Margaux would paint once more.

chapter 9

WHAT IS CHEATING?

Now we find ourselves in the knowledge of what is cheating. It is cheating to treat oneself as an object, or as an image to tend to, or as an icon. It was true four thousand years ago when our ancestors wandered the desert, and it's as true today when the icon is our selves.

The Jews wandered through the desert, thrown from the land, for as soon as we did settle, we made an idol to worship. Our punishment was to wander and be like gypsies without anything except the necessities for living, which we carried on our backs. So the story of wandering and being expelled is told, and is an old one.

There is no way we can be forgiven except to say: We did not even know how to talk to our own mothers. We were left with our friends, as lost as we were. We were left with ourselves, as lost as our friends—sheep with no shepherd,

sheared of whatever once kept us warm. We couldn't even
really believe that the sheep that came before us were warmed
by their own wool. It all seemed so improbable and far
away.

Now we are at the point where all the cards have been laid
and the story they chart can be read. We are worse off than
we were at the beginning—but this could have been predicted from our starting point. In the beginning, the gods
gave us liberty; in the end, we discovered cheating. Instead
of developing the capacities within, we took two roads: the
delusion and oblivion of drugs—which didn't start off as
cheating, but as access to the sublime; and treating ourselves as objects to be admired—the attempt to make the
self into an object of need and desire by tending to the
image of our selves. We have found that, in our freedom,
we have wanted to be like coke to the coke addict, food to
the starving person, and the middle of the night to thieves.
    Yet the three ways the art impulse can manifest itself are:
as an object, like a painting; as a gesture; and as a reproduction, such as a book. When we try to turn ourselves into a
beautiful object, it is because we mistakenly consider ourselves to *be* an object, when a human being is really the other
two: a gesture, and a reproduction of the human type. One
only has to travel on a subway during rush hour and pull
into a station and see all the people waiting to get on and
off to be struck by how many of us there actually are in the
world. One is a reproduction of the human type—one sleeps

like other humans, eats like other humans, loves like other humans, and is born and dies like all other humans. We are gestures, but we less resemble an original painting than one unit of a hundred thousand copies of a book being sold.

Now the gestures we chose are revealed as cheating. Instead of being, one appears to be. And the cheater breaks her own heart.

Yet the sex started off so incredibly sublime! The dinners, the nights, the paintings, my beauty, his beauty, hers, theirs. At first, the drugs gave us a feeling for the sublime in nature and ourselves. When we took them, we expanded into a thousand pieces. Then it seemed like cheating when we already were in a thousand pieces, and the sex and drugs didn't expand us into a hundred thousand more or put us back together again.

But in those early days on earth, nobody could have made a complaint against us.

chapter 10

WHAT IS DESTINY?

I continue to write *soul* as *sould*. It is my only consistent typo. My unease about it goes so deep that I try never to speak about it to anyone. Every time I write that word, I quickly erase the *d* and try not to think about it anymore. It's like when you hit a bird on an empty street at night— you just fix your eyes straight ahead and keep driving. No one saw you; it's between you and the bird. There's nothing to be done about it now—it happened.

Like *sould*. It happened. Nothing to be done about it now. Move on. Life is so short, and of all the questions I ask myself in this life, none should involve this typographical error, or whether in fact I have sold my soul, or had no soul to begin with to sell. I shouldn't dwell on it. Who gives a fuck in this fucked-up world. There are problems so vast and so deep that a young woman sitting alone in her room should slit her throat and die sooner than bother about the state of her soul, when so many great artists before her spent decades recalibrating a single blank canvas in their studio, fifteen, sixteen hours a day, as their marriages crumbled into the soil.

I know better than to let my life crumble around me just because somewhere inside me I am without a soul. For I sold it. And I don't remember to whom. Or why. Or when.

When I strip away my dreams, what I imagine to be my potential, all the things I haven't said, what I imagine I feel for other people in the absence of my expressing it, all the rules I've made for myself that I don't follow—I see that I've done as little as anyone else in this world to deserve the grand moniker *I*. In fact, apart from being the only person living in this apartment, I'm not sure what distinguishes me.

There are people whose learning is so great, they seem to inhabit a different realm of species-hood entirely. Somehow, they appear untroubled by the nullness. They are filled up with history and legends and beautiful poetry and all the gestures of all the great people down through time. When they talk, they are carried on a sea of their own belonging. It is like they were born to be fathers to us all. I should like one day to impale them all on a long stick. But I know I won't. It will never be one of the gestures by which I am known, so I might as well forget about it. Thinking about it does little to help me inhabit the realm of living.

. . .

Yet there is one character in history who is reassuring me these days: Moses. I hadn't realized until last week that in his youth he killed a man, an Egyptian, and buried him under some sand. The next day he saw two men fighting. When he tried to stop them, they said to Moses, "What? And if we don't—are you going to kill us too?" He became afraid. He thought, *Everyone knows what I have done.*

Then he fled town.

And he is king of the Jews—*my* king. If that is what my king is like, what can I expect for myself? If the king of my people had to be told by God to take off his shoes for he was standing on holy ground when God addressed him for the first time, I should not worry that I—who have never been addressed by God—am all the time standing on holy ground with running shoes on. I used to worry that I wasn't enough like Jesus, but yesterday I remembered who was my king: a man who, when God told him to lead the people out of Egypt, said, "But I'm not a good talker! Couldn't you ask my brother instead?" So it should not be so hard to come at this life with a little bit of honesty. I don't need to be great like the leader of the Christian people. I can be a bumbling murderous coward like the king of the Jews.

· *chapter 11* ·

THE BUS STATION

At the bus station, sitting on an orange, molded-plastic chair, I looked through a huge book called *Important Artists*—the only book I packed for my journey. I had borrowed it from Sholem a few months before. Now that I had no hope of finding my soul by staying where I was, I wanted to take a different route to the one thing that would justify the ugliness inside me: I would become Important.

I sat there with the book on my knees, moving carefully through the pages with a pink highlighting pen and a yellow one, like a beautiful, anxious, pregnant young mother studying for her medical school exams. I blew away a bit of sand that was stuck in the spine of the book.

Reading through the biographies and taking notes, I

learned that the artists originated in a hundred and eleven cities, but by the Important phase of their careers, they populated thirty-nine. Twenty-three of those cities had only one artist in them, and the remaining sixteen held the rest. Twenty-seven percent of the artists had left their country of birth. Not a single American-born artist had moved outside of America.

Of the sixteen cities where more than one Important Artist lived, six held only two artists who were Important: Buenos Aires, Rio, Vancouver, Leipzig, Tokyo, Cologne. I eliminated those six, for the odds were too small of becoming Important there, and I was left with only nine cities, where three or more Important Artists lived:

Glasgow	4
Düsseldorf	5
Mexico City	6
Paris	7
Amsterdam	8
Los Angeles	9
London	15
Berlin	19
New York	30

In the future, would the list say:

Toronto	3 ?

But I couldn't think like that now! I wasn't living in a future time—but the present time.

I paused for a moment before making my decision, cradling those only-one-Important-Artist cities in my heart, as if before putting them to their death: Antwerp, Vienna, Warsaw, Barcelona, San Fernando, Douarnenez, Helsinki, Port of Spain, Zurich, Havana, Frankfurt, Milan, Cairo, Tarnów, Las Palmas, Hermosa Beach, Seoul, Altadena, Matsudo City, Ho Chi Minh City, Santo Bello Jesus, Rheydt.

The answer was obvious: New York. It had been certain before I began. I could be there in twelve hours, for cheap, on the bus. There, the odds of meeting someone Important, and thus becoming Important myself, were best. I went to the counter. The lady told me that a bus would be leaving in exactly two hours. I handed her my credit card and signed a promise to pay eighty-nine dollars, and I put the ticket in my pocket.

I called Ryan and told him he could take over my apartment, since his was smaller than mine. Then I nervously called Israel and told him I was going to New York. When he asked me why, I said I was going there to finish my play. It was not true, but I hoped he would be really impressed. There was a pause on the other end.

Then he said, "I hope you write until your fucking fingers break."

. . .

Heading out of the station for a smoke, in pain, I passed two teenage girls who were standing with their bags before a deli, gazing up at its illuminated menu.

"What is American cheese anyway?" I heard one of them say.

Her friend replied, "I think it means it has a chemical in it."

· *chapter 12* ·

SHEILA WANDERS IN NEW YORK

I called Jen, who once put me up in France, and asked if I might stay with her my first few nights in New York while I looked for an apartment of my own. She had returned to America and, in her friendly way, agreed to help me. I was looking forward to seeing her and imagined us growing closer and becoming true friends.

On the bus ride down, I stared out the window and recalled the happy days we had spent together in Paris. We had gone to the Musée d'Orsay. I remembered standing at the far end of one of the galleries, looking for fifteen minutes at a tiny painting of a single stalk of asparagus. It was the most moving thing I had ever seen, painted so tenderly and with such a loose hand that it hardly seemed like it had been any work at all. When I finally looked over to see who had painted it, I discovered it was Manet, one of my favorite painters. I wondered at this; was there something in his hand or his soul—or elsewhere—that was essentially him, so much so that it compelled me every time, and made me love everything that was his, without even knowing it was?

When Jen and I left the building, I told her about my experience with the painting. Then she told me about her favorite painting: *Jacob Wrestling with the Angel*. As we walked through the fine, slightly damp Paris air, she explained why she liked it. "From my own point of view, when I am struggling, I always imagine I am struggling with a devil. But when I saw that painting I realized—no, it's an angel. Now I always try to remember, when I am struggling, that I am struggling with an angel.

"So you see, I'm really leery of these self-improvement seminars where you try to make yourself better and better. We probably need to suffer in order to . . . well, in order to break the spells."

I arrived at her apartment on the Lower East Side at ten the next morning, sweaty from the all-night bus ride and feeling the grime all over my flesh. It was a sunny day, and I carried my heavy suitcase though the subways and up into the street. I collected the keys at a deli near where she lived. Then I went into her apartment and lay down on her couch, which was made over with white sheets. There was

a note on the pillow from Jen. She said she would see me
after work. We had agreed that we would go out later that
night to see a lecture by an important young graphic novelist.

I lay there for a while with my eyes wide open. The
apartment was large and fancy, all done over in rich browns
and reds. It belonged to her wealthy boyfriend. She was
alone half the time—he often traveled. He was in the tech
industry, and she once told me that he had Asperger's syn-
drome. Then she reassured me that Silicon Valley boys
aren't so bad to sleep with because they've read all the
manuals.

That evening, we talked for a bit as Jen ate from the fridge
while I watched. I began to grow anxious. Time was passing, and it started to seem like we'd never leave the apartment. I wanted to be among the Important people! I was
worried that we were running late. I didn't want to spend
my whole time in New York in someone's apartment. I put
on my jacket, hoping Jen would get the hint, but instead
she showed me a present that her boyfriend had given her:
a stuffed, plush parrot that was perched on the edge of the
glass-topped dining table. She went and began twisting a
rubber cracker back and forth in its beak. "Eat, eat!" she said.
Finally I went and stood in the hallway. She followed me
there, but after picking up her purse, she glanced over her
shoulder at the parrot. She seemed anxious and regretful. "I

think it's still hungry," she said, and she hurried back to feed the plastic cracker into its mouth some more. I stood there leaning against the doorjamb, watching, exasperated. We remained in her apartment like that for the rest of the night.

I guess those were my early days in New York. But it's everyone's story, I know.

chapter 13

DESTINY REARS ITS UGLY HEAD

The next day, I wandered around the city, looking up at the buildings to see if I could find a place to rent. Earlier that morning, I had written an email to the theater, telling the producer to pull the play. She emailed within minutes and told me she was disappointed. I didn't care. As I walked the streets, I thought only about Israel.

There, in the sunlight, all of him went through me: how one afternoon, early, when he was still moved by me, he had pulled out from his closet a canvas he had made with just my name painted on it in a sea of purple, like a vagina opening, and after nakedly holding it before me for a moment, shyly returned it to his closet. Even I, with all the feelings I had for him, knew it was no good. He was a genius, but not a genius at painting. He was a genius at fucking. If he painted as well as he fucked, he would have had the whole world hanging him on their walls just to watch his cock and hips.

He had skin the color of tomatoes and eyes the color of mustard and ears the color of rabbit stew and feet the color of grass. And the smells from him were tomato and mustard and rabbit and grass. The words he spoke sounded like snakes in the grass. And when he smiled it was like mustard on the smile of a wound. When he touched me, my cells bred like rabbits: more blood, more flesh. All of my self came alive to breed to meet him doubly, triply; my body multiplied to satisfy him.

My eyes grew hot and welled up with hot tears as I considered our sex, for the first time, from his point of view. He would have gone home with the smell of my juices on his cock, and in the hairs around his cock, and he might have even put his hand there to find my smells and inhale them in the privacy of his own home, in his bed, and might have been intoxicated by it.

I had hardly told Margaux a word about him, for she was made impatient by conversations about relationships or men. Yet I had gone over to her apartment one afternoon, very early in my time with him, having not heard from him in forty-three hours, and paced around her kitchen like a wild animal until she decided to calm me down. She set me up in the other room, in front of her TV, and made me watch a movie while she painted in the next room. It was a French film, about love and bondage and sex. Well, I just emerged two hours later, into her studio, saying, near tears, "Love is a battle between the sexes in which the man always wins because that's more erotic for everyone!"

Not even turning, she said, "I should have shown you a different movie."

The next night I went with Jen to a party and there I met a beautiful girl named Anjali. She was thin-limbed and her dark hair was cut below her shoulders, and it was very clean and shiny. Her father was from France and her mother was from India, and she had lived in both places but was now living in New York. I liked her instantly, just the way that sometimes happens. There she was, with her bright, enthusiastic eyes, and we stood in the corner excitedly talking, and soon we were talking about love.

ANJALI

So I had decided I couldn't get into a relationship right then because it wouldn't be good for me—I needed to build myself up—enjoy my own company without sacrificing myself for someone else. I just wanted to have fun and be frivolous and air-headed and light, and just enjoy life and drink and go out and whatever, fuck. So I met this Italian guy at a party in Paris and we got on fine; at seven o'clock in the morning, we left—four people—a Pakistani, a Greek girl, he and I, and the party was really close to my house so I asked them if they wanted to come up and sleep at my place, because we were all tired.

SHEILA

Yeah?

ANJALI

Well, the Greek girl and the Pakistani guy decided to go home, but the Italian guy decided to come and sleep at my apartment. So he came up and we went to the balcony to have a cigarette, and he was feeling cold so we came back inside. We were sitting on the sofa next to each other, and he suddenly said, Actually, I think I'm going to go home. I was like, Okay. And he said, But give me your phone number and everything else. I gave him my phone number, really not thinking he was going to call or anything, and the next day he sent me a text message saying, *Listen, if you need any help doing little works in your house and stuff like that, give me a ring and I'll come and help you.*

SHEILA

(*embarassed*) Oh, that's nice!

ANJALI

I wrote him back and said, I don't need any material help, but if you want to go and have a coffee, sure.

Both laugh.

SHEILA

Such a funny offer!

ANJALI

So we went to have lunch, and he told me about his sentimental life, which was really, really complicated—

SHEILA

(*giggling*) His sentimental life?

ANJALI

That's how you say it in French, *la vie sentimentale*—his love
life.

SHEILA

Oh, that's nice.

ANJALI

He started telling me about how he'd been for so many
years with this girl, and he loved her and she loved him,
and she wanted absolutely to have a child and he didn't. He
couldn't deal with this concept of paternity, so she said,
Okay. She left him, and within the next year she got pregnant. She met someone else. She has a baby. And he's still
trying to sort out his problems with paternity. In the mean-
time, he met a much younger girl, and, um, he's the kind of
guy who likes to play daddy and she needed a daddy, but
now he's like, Okay, I can't play daddy anymore, because I
have to sort out this thing about being a father, and I have
to learn about becoming the daddy of a child and not a
woman, so I'm going to move to Paris for a year and think

about all of this. So this is the state this poor guy is in! And he tells me this—

Sheila laughs.

And I'm like, Listen, on Saturday night, why didn't you—I mean, you came to my flat and twenty minutes after you left. What happened? Were you afraid? And he was a bit taken aback by my being so direct, and he was like, Yes, I was scared. I really wanted to kiss you, and that scared me so I left. And I was like, Oh well, that's too bad. You should have kissed me first and *then* left.

They laugh.

SHEILA

Maybe he's very sensitive, and he thinks he's going to fall in love with you.

ANJALI

But isn't that like—

SHEILA

—a woman?

ANJALI

Yes! The men in France are really messed up. They're all afraid of women. They're not ready for commitment and paternity—which some women would be asking from them—so they don't want to get involved with this, let's say, mother kind of woman. Then at the same time, the one who would be a mistress kind of woman or a slut is too overbearing. She's going to be controlling the whole situation, and that scares him. That's why there's suddenly this big increase in homosexuality. I mean, there's always been homosexuality in France, but now it's just like, Okay, it's simpler to be with a man because I don't have to deal with these issues.

SHEILA

Really? You think it's that easy to become a—a—to be a homosexual?

ANJALI

Oh, in France, yes.

SHEILA

But I mean—for a human being? For a man? Just to sort of shift his—

ANJALI

I don't know if he's shifting his libido, but he's definitely shifting his . . . uh . . . his area of risk taking. They feel the suffering involved with a man is less.

After the party, Jen and I emerged into the streets. I felt excited for more life and in love with Anjali, certain for good things to come. The air was warm and it was not so late, so we went to the second night of the graphic novelist's talk. We sat in the auditorium and watched the graphic novelist up there on the stage. At one point, answering a question from the audience, he said that people often approached him at public appearances and sort of asked or wondered or complained about the fact that they were not as good at drawing as he was, even though they worked so hard. They would put the question to him: what did he have that was so special? Usually they were in their early thirties—his age. And always he would talk with them, and it would become clear that most of these people had only started drawing three or four years ago—so what could he say? He had started drawing seriously at the age of two.

As Jen and I walked home together, she brought up her uneasy feelings, stirred by the talk. He represented exactly the sort of person who made her feel really bad about her life and sort of despairing. She worried that she would never be good enough at anything. She had spent most of her life wondering where her father was, and her twenties going to parties and sleeping with men. She had not chosen a line of work early and stuck with it and gotten good.

I really wanted to make her feel better. Summoning everything within me, I said, "So what if you haven't been drawing comics since the age of two. *Who cares?* I'm convinced that everybody has been doing *something* since the age of two. And I'll bet the genius is not the person who has been drawing comics since the age of two, but the person who, since the age of two, has been wondering where her father is . . ."

Then Jen began to walk with a lighter step, and I did too.

Late that night, back at Jen's, Sheila gets an email from Israel . . .

1. hey Slut,
2. so theres something i need done for me.
3. i want you to go out, this weekend or next, doesnt matter, wearing a short skirt and no panties. go to a well-attended bar or patio.
4. you are going to write me a letter, in pen on paper. the letter will be in the style of a letter home from a first-year university student or camper.
5. you will tell me in the letter how much you miss my cum in your mouth and how you feel you deserve to come home and please me for the rest of the summer.
6. you will write also about how my cock has changed your life.

1. while you are writing this, i want your legs spread apart so if someone was looking, they could see your wet cunt.
2. pick someone on the patio that you feel deserves to see your cunt, like an old man. be very coy about the whole thing, dont let on that you know he can see your cunt.
3. just keep writing and look up every once in a while to see if he is looking.
4. act very naturally, and when you are done with the letter mail it to me.

The blood in my arms ran cold.

chapter 14

SHEILA WANDERS IN THE COPY SHOP

The next morning I went out. I went to get some stationery, stamps, and a pen. I wandered for fifteen blocks before I noticed—in the window of the basement of a brownstone—a tan piece of cardboard on which was written, in thick black marker: COPY SHOP. Beneath it was a line drawing of a matzo and four words: WE SELL BIRD'S MILK. Bird's Milk had been my father's favorite treat! My mother fed it to him in the early years of their marriage. It was a custard soup with egg white clouds floating on top. I knew this place was calling me like fate; that it would have just what I needed.

I went down the steps and entered a room that was long and cramped. The walls were all shelves, and from the shelves spilled ink, paper, pens, glue, staplers, rulers, and some items I didn't know. Near the back of the store was a tiny, cluttered desk with a very old computer on it, and above the computer were pasted colored notes in Hebrew. Behind the desk was a tiny office space, sectioned off by half a wall. Boxes were stacked everywhere. A man appeared from amid the dust: balding, not tall, in a torn sweater and beige pants. He had a round, smooth face and tiny eyes, and he stared at me as I moved through the clutter.

"I saw your sign about Bird's Milk," I said.

"Do you even know what it *means*?" he asked in an aggrieved and accusatory tone. "Do you even know what Bird's Milk *is*?"

I replied that it was my father's favorite dessert.

"What? No! They hang these signs over shopkeeper's stalls in Prague! *We Sell Bird's Milk* means *We Sell Everything*!"

He cleared his throat in disgust, but he clearly wanted to talk more, for then he said, "I'm a Jew. I was born as a Jew. By the way, a Jew is a Jew. Did you know that? Even if you convert to another religion, you are still a Jew."

SHEILA

Yeah, I think so.

SOLOMON

There's nothing to think! This is our religion!

SHEILA

If you have a mother who's a Jew.

SOLOMON

Tell me how come if your mother is Jewish and not the father.

SHEILA

Because you know who the mother is, but you don't know
who the father is.

SOLOMON

Ah, that's bullshit.

SHEILA

You don't know who—necessarily who the father is!

SOLOMON

That's bullshit. That's complete bullshit.

SHEILA

'Cause the father passes on the cultural Judaism, he teaches
the laws, but the mother passes on the—

SOLOMON

No, no, it's complete nonsense.

SHEILA

What do you mean it's nonsense?

SOLOMON

It's nonsense because that's not how Judaism was in ancient
times! There was a change between the sixth and the ninth
centuries on the subject.

SHEILA

Why did they change it?

SOLOMON

A-*ha*! Here we are! *Why?*

SHEILA

Well?

SOLOMON

There's a good reason.

SHEILA

Tell me.

SOLOMON

I don't know.

SHEILA

You don't *know*? You know *when* it happened, but you don't know *why*?

SOLOMON

It's one of the hottest conversations in Jewish scholarship in the last twenty—

SHEILA

And what are the speculations?

SOLOMON

The speculations? Nobody knows why! There's actually no answer. It's nothing to do with genetics.

SHEILA

So you're saying there was a change between the sixth and ninth centuries. It changed from the father passing on the religion, to the mother—

SOLOMON

I think personally it has to do with the occupation.

SHEILA

What occupation?

SOLOMON

Of the fathers.

SHEILA

What do you mean the occupation of the fathers?

SOLOMON

What the fathers *did*!

SHEILA

Elaborate.

SOLOMON

What did the Hungarians *do*? How do we have Hungarians? Where do Hungarians *come from*?

SHEILA

From Hungary.

SOLOMON

No, no! They don't come from Hungary!

SHEILA

What do you mean! Just explain what you mean by the occupation of the fathers. You mean what they were occupied with—or is it that they were occupied?

SOLOMON

But you see, nobody really knows. Why, in that period of time, does this drastic change occur? There's no answer.

SHEILA

But doesn't it make sense? If the fathers aren't around, who's going to transmit the traditions and the culture to the children except the mothers?

SOLOMON

The mothers cannot do that because they aren't that learned.

SHEILA

But the women are the ones who run the holidays, so they

know the traditions. They're the ones who cook. I know it from my own family. So it makes sense that the women would know the traditions from growing up in their families—and that they would pass it on to their children.

SOLOMON

By the way, it's a good possibility what you say. I'm not saying that what you're saying is completely false—

SHEILA

I don't know if it's nonsense or true, but it makes sense.

SOLOMON

Logically, logically. But that's not the reason.

SHEILA

Then what's the reason?

SOLOMON

That's not the reason.

SHEILA

What's the reason?

SOLOMON

That's not the reason.

SHEILA

What's the reason?

SOLOMON

I don't know.

SHEILA

Then how can you say that's not the reason!

SOLOMON

Because it *cannot* be the reason.

SHEILA

Why!

SOLOMON

It cannot be the reason! In order for a drastic change like this, in a male-dominated religion like Judaism, for something like the mothers passing on the religion to happen, there had to be something drastic. We are missing something in this puzzle. (*to a delivery man*) How you doing? (*turning back*) By the way, there's a guy at Yale who has been trying to write about it, but up to now we don't have any good explanation—

DELIVERY MAN

How do you spell?

SOLOMON

SOLOMON, it's S-O-L-O-M-O-N—no good explanation on that subject. It's very critical to understand this thing. There's no explanation by the rabbis, either.

Now, I'll explain to you what the problem is. When the state of Israel was established in '48, there was a decision not to write a constitution. Do you think that's good or bad?

SHEILA

Do they plan to write a constitution eventually?

SOLOMON

Well, when the Messiah will come. What do you think about that?

SHEILA

How are they going to live until then? By what principles?

SOLOMON

The principles of—God knows. Their *own* principles!

SHEILA

Individual principles?

SOLOMON

I have no idea! Jews know best. They know better than anybody else how to live.

SHEILA

(*laughing*) They have the covenant with God.

SOLOMON

You have to—thinking is a very complex thing. Thinking is something that is not done anymore. You understand? Thinking is something that is not done anymore, because we've stopped thinking, because if people were thinking, we wouldn't have gotten ourselves into the trouble we have gotten ourselves into.

SHEILA

But people have always gotten themselves into trouble.

SOLOMON

Never mind that. Anyway, so what you have is a judicial disaster, and because of that judicial disaster, we have all the wars that you see now. Because of their inability to write a constitution, they ruined their chances for survival. That is my theory—my philosophical theory. If you don't write a book by which you're going to rule yourself, you are opening the door to all kinds of things that only God knows. Do you know that there's not a single record in all of Egyptian history of Jews working there as slaves?

SHEILA

So you think it's a lie?

SOLOMON

That's not what I said. Why would I say!—it has nothing to do with a lie or not!

SHEILA

So why wouldn't they write it down? Probably they
think it was important.

SOLOMON

No, no, I'm talking about the Egyptians.

SHEILA

Yes, but why talk about one's slaves?

SOLOMON

Why not? They make hieroglyphs of everything
world. I mean, they decorated hieroglyphs—

SHEILA

But maybe one's slaves are below one's consciousness

SOLOMON

No, but the king stands there, and there's seven th
slaves. Why shouldn't they show them? They show
other things.

SHEILA

Do they show the insects?

SOLOMON

Absolutely! Insects are very important!

SOLOMO

Don't touch those things.

SHEILA

What's this book?

SOLOMO

Don't touch—that's my private st
don't touch things here becaus
becomes a, a, a—

SHEILA

A mess.

SOLOMON

A mess, and you cannot, becaus
things either. But anyway. So wh

SHEILA

(*puts the book down*) I want to knov
the desert versus what it's like to t

A young man has been vacantly regard

SOLOMON

Sir, can I help you with somethin

YOUNG MA

Do you have pens?

SOLOMON

Yes. Do you have money?

YOUNG MAN

Of course.

SOLOMON

What kind of pen do you want? Do you want something to enrich your mind, or something to enrich your pocket?

YOUNG MAN

(*pause*) I just want something that writes well.

SOLOMON

Well, okay.

Solomon takes something from his desk.

What about this one? It's a gel pen.

YOUNG MAN

A gel pen.

SHEILA

It's good. I just got one. I like it far more.

SOLOMON

Oh, God.

SHEILA

It's a good pen!

YOUNG MAN

How much is it?

SOLOMON

How much do you want to pay?

YOUNG MAN

A dollar.

SOLOMON

Two dollars. It sells for two-fifty.

YOUNG MAN

Okay, I'll take one.

SOLOMON

What a deal. (*yelling to his wife in the back*) Enid, we make two dollars! So what do you want to do when you grow up?

YOUNG MAN

I was hoping I was almost grown up.

SOLOMON

You know we never grow up. I hope you realize that. What do you study?

YOUNG MAN

Uh . . . computer stuff.

SOLOMON

We are in the beginning of the revolution—the computer revolution! Or evolution. I think they're eventually going to make people who are computers in China . . .

The young man exits the shop.

Now, there's a lot of things that don't connect. I'll give you an example. I was in Tel Aviv at the university and I met this guy, he's writing a book about those missing thousand years. You know what my favorite subject is?

SHEILA

Israel.

SOLOMON

What is an Israeli? It's my nationality. I actually wrote a preamble to the Israeli constitution. I'll give it to you to read. Takes five minutes. You'll figure it out. As an intelligent woman, you'll figure it out in three minutes. Now I'll tell you why Martin Buber is an idiot.

SHEILA

I've got one more thing to say!

SOLOMON

No! No! No!

SHEILA

I've got one more thing to say! Have you heard of Margaret Mead?

SOLOMON

Absolutely, I love her. We're going to do some anthropology in a minute. We're going into it.

SHEILA

Listen to what Margaret Mead said: "The major task of every civilization is to get the fathers involved in the child-rearing process."

Pause.

SOLOMON

(*calling*) Enid! Enid! Enid!

ENID

(*calling, bored*) What?

SOLOMON

Did you hear what she said about Margaret Mead? You know, tell her that I failed Lamaze!

ENID

(*calling*) He was the only one.

SHEILA

He's the only one to have failed Lamaze? How do you fail
Lamaze?

ENID

(*calling*) Chickening out!

SHEILA

Chickening out?

SOLOMON

By the way—Margaret Mead on that issue is a complete
failure.

SHEILA

Why?

SOLOMON

Because she's a complete failure! Because I'll tell you—
listen. The issue is like this. So with the waves that come
from near China, Mongolia—you know what comes? Sha-
manism. Do you know what a shaman is?

SHEILA

A spiritual—

SOLOMON

A man who connects between you and God, and also a
healer. Do you know that I'm a shaman?

SHEILA

Okay.

SOLOMON

Did you know that? I'm a healer. I'm actually officially a
healer.

SHEILA

What does it mean to fail Lamaze?

SOLOMON

Leave it. It's childbirth. We studied it when Enid was pregnant. We went to the hospital to study this thing. It's just—I
couldn't take it.

He takes a deep breath.

Anyway. It's complete nonsense. She gave birth without me
there. Ehm, anyway. The issue is not that thing. The issue
is something different.

I left the copy shop frustrated and upset. He was just another
man who wanted to teach me something.

chapter 15

WHAT IS EMPATHY?

Flustered and feeling like I was running out of time, I hurried down to a restaurant near the river—to a patio that was high-end and touristy and packed with people. The tables were wrought iron, and the cloth napkins were black. Families were there, and young couples, and when I arrived everyone was sipping cold drinks and eating large salads.

A waitress met me at the entrance and seated me near the middle of the restaurant, and I ordered a Campari and soda, then brushed some grains of sand from the table. I looked around to see who was near, to determine the best way to arrange myself. At a short distance, maybe ten feet away, I noticed an older man. He was dignified and wore a navy blue suit and hat. His shirt was heavily starched, and his white cuffs peeked out from beneath his heavy suit. Where a gap opened between his pant cuffs and socks, I could see the hair on his legs. He had a newspaper folded in front of him and a coffee by his side, and I thought about Israel's email: *pick someone on the patio that you feel deserves to see your cunt, like an old man.* Why not this man, of all men?

I took a gulp of my drink and rummaged in my bag for the paper and pen I had bought. My face began to flush with excitement as I spread apart my legs and looked down at the blank page before me, trying to behave as though this was the most natural thing in the world. I knew I was supposed to be very nonchalant about the whole thing. I put my pen in my mouth, then took it out and began to write.

I tried to compose something that would show how perfect and willing I was—still was, even though I had left—and how accommodating and devoted I could be. I really tried to write it in such a way that it would turn Israel on even more than a letter from a real teenage camper would.

I was about three pages into a detailed explanation of how his cock had changed my life, when an odd sensation began creeping through me, an awareness of how sick it was that all this time I had been having so much trouble writing my play, yet instead of laboring away at it, here I was writing this fucking letter—this cock-sucking letter of flattery for Israel!

I glanced up and saw that the man across from me had gone, and in his place sat a chubby young boy—and he laughed up at me openly to see my whole cunt. My throat caught and my eyes leapt to his parents, and, flushing red, I fumbled out some bills and threw them on the table and shoved my glass on top of them and hurried away.

I pushed past people as I made my way quickly from there, my head bent low, heart thumping, looking only at the street. Tears blurred my eyes, and trees crashed into cars. My mind swirled far and fast, and a painting of Eli Langer's came with great force into my head—a painting from that fateful show: a naked little girl with a round little tummy sits astride the neck of an older man, who lies there naked on his back, on a bed. Her legs hug either side of his neck, and her pussy is front and center, right below his chin. *She should not be sitting there like that!*

As the painting filled me, I began to see that the worst thing about child abuse would be the empathy you would have for the grown-up, who feels compelled to do these things. Worse would be the tenderness you would feel for the adult because you love them—because you believe they are being forced by something inside of them to do these terrible things. You would want to help them—to make them feel better—and you would help them feel better by complying, and complying without judgment. To do otherwise would leave you guilty for making them feel so bad. But the next thing that would happen is you would confuse their desire with yours—but your desire would be to love, not for the act itself. Forever after, though, it would be really hard to untangle how you imagined other people wanted you to behave from how *you* wanted to behave. How would you even know what you wanted, when at such a young age, desire had been all mixed up with empathy and guilt?

How could I castrate my mind—neuter it!—and build up a resistance to know what was mine from what was everyone else's, and finally be in the world in my *own* way? That endless capacity for empathy—which you have to really kill in order to act freely, to know your own desires!

Did I want to write this letter to Israel because I *wanted* to? Did I want to lead the people out of bondage because it was a desire I had absorbed from the world, or my own religious history? Is that why I wanted to finish the play? Why had I even taken it on? Why had I come to New York? Had my every act, all along, just been guilt-drenched empathy for the perversions of the world?

Turning onto Jen's street, I grew suddenly dizzy and stopped to rest my hand against a pole. I could have vomited. I saw it all so clearly: I had come to New York as a student, like it was my teacher. And hadn't I *always* gone into the world making everyone and everything a lesson in how I should be? Somehow I had turned myself into the worst thing in the world: I was just another man who wanted to teach me something!

chapter 16

WHAT IS LOVE?

I had no idea how it had come to this, or what I needed to do to fix what was inside me. I saw how upside down my life had become—that I had become the thing I hated. But what could make it better?

I could not stay at Jen's any longer. I took my bags and left a farewell note and went to the bus station. I bought a ticket heading to Atlantic City. I wanted to be near the sea.

That night, I walked along the boardwalk, then stepped off the boardwalk and walked shoeless through the sand. I tried my best to remain silent and not ask myself any questions, nor look around for someone to answer questions for me. I sat down in the sand and looked out at the waves. It was so terrible to be alone. I felt how heavy my brain was in my head with all the questions that had been repeating for years.

Above me, the seagulls were lifted across a sky that was dark with night and clouds. In the distance, it was brighter blue where the clouds broke. Before me, the ocean was the color of steel. The waves were coming up onto the shore and pulling themselves back from the shore. I felt exhausted with how long the sea had been doing that for—always, without end. It didn't make sense that they had been washing up and away ever since the world first began. How could the waves do it, through each and every moment, and so naturally, as if it was for the first time, as if it was for the last time, as if it was for the middle time, as if it would go on forever, and as if it would one day end. The sea moved forward and back with all these possibilities, and all of them were true. Yet it didn't grow tired of itself the way I did. Why not?

Who cares? There would be no answers for me ever. I wanted to lose everything I ever had, or win back everything I had ever lost. I began to make my way to the casinos.

I was no man on a mountaintop like in a Caspar David Friedrich painting, made sublime by the sublimity around me—by the awesomeness of the ocean I was leaving behind. It was the opposite and would always be the opposite. I walked up the boardwalk and stopped where all the casinos stood.

I sat down at the slots and lost. I went to the roulette table and lost. I put fifty on red, and I lost.

I was not in the mood to speak to anyone. The last thing I wanted was to be with a man, but it could not be avoided for long, sitting at a bar as I was. Soon I was approached by a middle-aged fellow, with an East Indian accent and a nice, kind face—though I was not in the mood for even the kindest face. He sat down beside me and smiled, held out his hand, and said his name was Ron. I said, "Do you think everyone goes to heaven, or do some people go to hell?"

RON

I don't believe a loving father who created you is judgmental.

SHEILA

No?

RON

God is a care-loving father, like your own care-loving father. Why would he put you in hell when you make a mistake? As the Bible says, in Psalms 91: *I will hear them before they call me.* That means if you believe in God, he's already taken care of you. You might not understand it at that moment, but as the course of time passes, you will realize, *Oh, what happened was the best for me.* I am always feeling guidance. And if something goes wrong—I tell God, *You know more than me, you're in charge of the situation. I just leave it to you.* That's the best feeling. And you move on. Something will come up right on time. When I talk to God, God listens to me. When I was lost up north in the Michigan jungles—

SHEILA

In the jungles of—?

RON

Up north there was a wooded place. I got lost and I said, "Lord, help me." It was a snowy area. I didn't know how to get out. I said, "Lord, I need help." Suddenly I see a man hunting. That man said, "Oh, it's right here. Just go like that."

Pause.

All moments are like that in different ways.

Sheila notices his wedding band.

SHEILA

Is your wife your soul mate?

RON

(*hesitates*) No. She's not. I have a very, very humorous, very loving friendship with my son. I think this is the reason I am with her.

SHEILA

That's the reason you think you are with your wife—for your son?

RON

I think so. I think so.

SHEILA

Can a *son* be a soul mate? Could your soul mate be your son?

RON

(*brightening*) You know what? Maybe. Maybe! (*pause, frowns*) But with a woman you have sex. I think sex is very important in life. In other words, intimacy, loving, hugging, kissing. But—what are you drinking?

SHEILA

Scotch.

He orders her a scotch.

RON

Loving, hugging, and kissing. But that's not all. Walking, talking, fighting, loving each other. Fun in life. And to be with—you know—you're my wife—you're not at home—I keep calling, "Hey! Where you at?" I come home. "Where are you?" An element of missing something. *Where'd she go?*

SHEILA

You feel the missing of the person?

RON

Yes.

SHEILA

Does your wife miss you when you are gone?

RON

She never said that. Her way of thinking is different from how I think.

SHEILA

What's her way of thinking?

RON

I never understood. That's why I'm sad. This is why I drink. Maybe.

SHEILA

Uh, so if your wife is not your soul mate, do you think there's someone who is?

RON

I think I have met my soul mate, but I am not with her.

SHEILA

Oh.

RON

I don't know it, but I'm just telling you—deep in my heart. (*drinks*) If you meet a soul mate, it's one of the most beautiful, pleasurable things in life. I have seen soul mates. They never get away from each other. But with *not* a soul mate— they never get along.

SHEILA

(*puffs*) This is the worst eight-dollar cigar that's ever been sold to me.

RON

Do you live here?

SHEILA

No.

RON

Why don't you stay tonight?

SHEILA

I can't.

RON

Or tomorrow night.

SHEILA

I can't. (*puffs*) Why did you come to Atlantic City?

RON

Meeting women.

SHEILA

Meeting women?

RON

Nah, not necessarily. Enjoying nature. Meeting women and men. Very interesting people. Meeting human beings. Looking at the animals. And enjoying God's nature—very important. Get deep breathing exercises and think about God. Meditations.

Long pause as he drinks. Ron puts down his drink.

She is not my soul mate. My soul mate I met two years ago. God forgives me for it, I think. God understands. I do not think my wife thinks that I am her soul mate. She has never said anything about it. Do you think it is right . . . *six years*? For a woman not to sleep with a man? She is not my soul mate. Your soul mate is the one that misses you.

Sheila stops puffing on her cigar.

Alone that night in my tiny hotel room, under the scratchy duvet, my window facing the parking lot with the rusty cars and a blue light shining in, I slept deeply and I had a dream. I dreamed I was sailing on a boat in water, and coming to land, I got off and climbed a grassy mountain, at the top of which lay a massive graveyard. I looked about me for my task. Then I saw it—an ivory box. I held it in my hands and spent a very long time looking at it—its geometric pattern, interlaced with different shapes, perfectly symmetrical around all four sides. The box had a funny weight to it, at once light and heavy. I took it with me to the cliff's edge.

I knelt down and started digging at the ground with my nails—but then I paused and stopped. I went to another site and started digging there. But again I felt I might be digging in the entirely wrong place, so I got up and began digging elsewhere, here and there, until the sun started setting over the hill. I knew I was running out of time and that I could not delay anymore, so I dug a small hole and reached behind me for the box. Then I opened it. Glancing up at me was Margaux's head, severed from her body, her eyes open and darting around, scared.

I felt a horror so deep. Taking her head from the box, I threw it hard in the hole, then filled it up with dirt as her eyes kept blinking. I didn't want to see it. I knew I was a terrible person. I had not the will or courage to bury her whole body. I had desecrated her. Everyone knew I had only enough strength to bury her head.

When I woke in the morning, I knew only one thing—my one real duty in the world. I told myself, without hesitation, *Go home.*

chapter 17

EXODUS

I haven't found my suitcase yet. I don't know where I put it. I suppose I will find it, then I'll set off. God didn't send Moses into the desert by himself. He sent Moses with all of his people. So I'll go, be among them, smile widely so no one can see how hard it is for me.

So what if I wasn't called? If only a fortune teller hadn't told me that I was a leader, when it turns out I am a follower. How hard it will be to adjust my insides, when for so long I have been preparing for the role of leader in the smallest, most humiliating of ways. Every time I would pass a mirror I would glance into it at a jaunty angle, to make sure my jaw was set in such a way that would inspire the people's trust. Every morning, brushing my teeth, I'd look into my eyes and try to communicate an imperious attitude—to intimidate *myself*! I tried to get people to like me so that when the time came, they would be able to say to themselves, under their breaths, all impressed, *Whoa, I never thought it would be* her, *but okay, I get it.* I wanted to make impressions on those I would never meet again, so they might one day say, *Oh yeah, I met her once. I remember, sure—I might not have expected it, but I can totally see it now.*

Perhaps in ten years I'll be able to look back and see why it was better to be just one of the gang. Still, it's no fun playing the piccolo in the band. It's no great shakes being the dancer over at the *side* of the stage, when all the best performers stand in the middle of the stage, microphone in hand. It doesn't make me beloved to have had sex with a few hot guys. It has never pleased me how slowly I read. In fact, when I think about it, nothing in my life signaled out that I'd be the one. I don't know why I thought it.

Soon we are going. Soon we'll ship off. And I won't whisper to anyone, *I thought it was going to be me!*

I stood in line for the Greyhound, then got on the bus headed for Toronto and stored my suitcase in the tiny over-head rack and found a seat by the window, alone. I brushed the sand from the seat and sat down. After five minutes the bus driver turned on the engine, and we pulled into the morning's traffic and joined its heavy flow.

There had been rain in the air all morning, and the inside of the bus had a steamy feeling; soon there was the smell of bodies in the air. With the condensation on the windows, I could not see the trees passing fast. I could not see the road.

Lulled like a baby, and exhausted from my dreams the night before, I burrowed into sleep.

Awaking to my surroundings, I noticed the bus was pulling into Gravenhurst, where it always stopped on the way to the city, to allow everyone a quick lunch. I exited the bus with the others and followed them into a lineup for sandwiches at the old, side-of-the-road restaurant. The driver stood outside the bus smoking a cigarette.

There was nothing I wanted more than a grilled cheese sandwich, and I ordered it with a coffee. I was so looking forward to a really cheesy one—a grilled cheese sandwich just oozing with cheese. I thought about it as I waited, then accepted from the man at the counter a white paper plate, with a sandwich wrapped in foil that was white on the outside and silvery on the inside to keep it really warm.

Outside on the picnic bench I eagerly unwrapped the sandwich, but when I bit into it, it was soggy, and there was almost no cheese. It was not what I wanted, not what I had been picturing, but I adjusted myself to the reality of it. *Better to have a good imagination than a good grilled cheese sandwich*, I told myself.

Then, thinking of Margaux: *Better to have your failure right in front of you than the fantasy in your head.*

· *chapter 18* ·

WHAT IS BETRAYAL?

Back in my apartment, I went into the shower and washed everything away, until the sand ran down the drain. Then I stood on the bathroom floor, dripping naked. Outside the door, Ryan was packing up his things.

I felt so tired. The entire ride home I had been rehearsing in my head what I would say to Margaux: that she would not have to worry—I would never write about her again. I had given up the play for good—had given up trying. I wanted her to believe that in time, things would recalibrate inside her and she would come to trust in painting, and herself as a painter, again.

But for now, all I wanted was to sleep. I had been in the bus only fourteen hours, but it had felt like fourteen days.

· · ·

Before going to bed, I sat in the kitchen, wrapped in a towel, and went through my mail. There was an envelope that had been dropped off, with no stamp. My name was written on it in Margaux's hand, and it was dated earlier that week.

1. Dear Sheila,
2. I am sitting in our studio, furious. I can't help feeling like you have betrayed me.
3. To be my closest friend and record me, then as soon as you've learned how a person should be, you're done with me!
4. Now that you've gotten somewhere, your search is over, and that means the end of our friendship for you.
5. I always feared that one day you would forget why we wanted to see each other all the time, once you no longer felt it or wanted to, and that you would be resentful that I still wanted to see you.
6. Why would you still hang out with me? You're already off to the next thing that will help you be a genius.
7. But I cannot be your sometime friend.
8. That means I cannot be your friend at all.

I lay in bed and thought of cutting my wrists in the shower. I wanted to shoot myself in the face with a gun that released so many bullets at once, which would fan out and hit every part of my face and explode it into nothing, into mush. I tried to relax, but I could not because itchiness and heat were all over me everywhere. There was nothing in me that did not mourn. I knew I would always lose what was good. That was the kind of person I would always be. I could not believe the ripping, unbreathable pain in me, the shaking knot that twisted itself into my lower back, the ache in my jaw. There was nothing but this feeling, and the love of Margaux, which I had known, but now the dark back of Margaux, which is all I would ever know; the last I would see of her as she walked away, remembering how generous she had been when I was deserving.

As I slept that night I saw a room on the twelfth floor of a building with a courtyard in the center, and in this building lived young people and social workers, educators, lots of people. And into a room at the top there came deliveries of sharp, long knives, short knives, twisted knives, all sorts of knives, guns, ropes, and huge shipments of drugs. Razors were sent there, picks, files, cuffs, scissors, things to pull with, things to clamp with, and chains, everything like that, so that no one who saw the shipment and loved their sister could leave her there in that room with those boys, and yet someone *did*. Lots of people did. One person took the elevator down and told the social workers, "I'm scared. I think something might happen to my sister! I think something might be going on in that room!" But the social workers did not understand; one said she was going to go up, but she was not as scared as the person who left her sister, who just stood there pacing, beyond worrying, so certain, on the

main floor in the center of that courtyard. Because it would
now be too late. The social worker went up, but it was too
late because more boys had gone up with all their frighten-
ing clothes on, all their paint, all the things they dressed in
regularly to scare people. They went up, and the room got
more and more crowded with people who thought they
should take part in the orgy because why not join in for
once? Why always remain aloof? Why not join in and stick
the things, the metal bars, into the mouths? They wanted
to have a good time. The room was small, but it held all the
women you could think of and all the men you were ever
scared of in your whole life, passing on the street or just
imagining, and all the men you loved the most. That is
when the party started. So many of these people were
crowding in from the elevator that the social worker could
hardly make her way into the room, and she never did make
her way into the room, but came back with a pale face, her
hair frizzed with fear from not being let into this room
with all the tools and all the drugs, and that is where the
orgy began. That is where it began in no innocence at all,
but compared to what was to come, it began in innocence.
There were knives and girls skinned alive and kept alive,
and one woman screaming but trying to laugh it off to
another, "Look what they did to my face!"—and there were
the amputations performed right there, the limbs cut off, and
the bars fucked with in the mouth, and all the things that
can be done to a person including the pulling and ripping
of everything that we don't even know we love about a
person—their intactness, their perfect intactness—and all

the things that seem to us the person—they were destroyed, ripped away, so that you could not tell one girl from the other except that some were taller, some were thinner, but you could not see it in the face, just bloodiness, like animals turned inside out. And in the courtyard, and in the balconies surrounding all twelve floors of the courtyard was the whole audience; rowdy, unhappy guys who were waving their flags and watching and waiting, so that at every floor they had their paint—orange, yellow, purple, blue—and when they were done with the girls, and when they were still doing them, doing everything before they dropped each girl, one by one, to her terror, thrown from the room, twelve floors down to the concrete floor of the courtyard, blood falling off her body as she fell—no skin, no face, but kept alive—then from the balconies came the colors flung, and she would fall through eleven floors of thick paint, house paint and wall paint, burning at her skin that was no longer skin—a nice bright green, a happy yellow, orange, purple, red, a rainbow.

I had hurt Margaux beyond compare. The heat of shame was the heat of my body. There was not one cell in my body unsullied by what I had done.

chapter 19

IN FRONT OF THE BIKINI STORE

The next day, I woke late in the afternoon, and with a sinking heart remembered Margaux's letter. I did not want to go over, yet I had to go. I knew I had to go as soon as I could, even though I did not know the right thing to say. I made myself walk the three blocks to her place, my hair stringy and hanging low, nothing but nothing in my eyes.

I knocked on the door and saw her come down the stairs. When she opened the door, her mouth was down-turned. Her hair was in triangles, as if she had just woken, and she came onto the stoop.

She said, "I called you and you were gone. I went to your house and you'd left. How could you leave me when things were so hard? You left without even saying good-bye!"

I braced my body, became as tight and hard as armor. I felt nothing but the need to get through this and over it.

"But it was me who made them hard! I thought I would leave so that things could be better for you! So you could forget what I had done."

"After I searched high and low and found you! All my life all I wanted was a girl! And then when I needed her, she disappeared."

I started to cry. "But I was so bad I made it so you couldn't paint anymore!"

"Look, I agreed to be taped. But you—you figured out how a person should be and then you went to New York to be it!"

"No! Besides, I'm not using the recordings or anything like that. I gave up the play."

"Great! So it was all meaningless. All that we went through was for nothing."

I put my face in my hands. I had thought, in saying this, that it would make things better, but it only made her more upset.

It took forty years for the Israelites to get from Egypt to the banks of the Jordan, a journey that should have taken days. It was no accident. That generation had to die. They could not enter the promised land. A generation born into slavery is not ready for the responsibilities of freedom.

Pacing through our neighborhood, I spotted Sholem in the window of his favorite coffee shop, sketching on paper, looking glum. I went in and asked if I could sit with him for a bit. He said okay. I wanted to tell him about my life and ask for his advice, but he immediately started talking about his life. He said that a few weeks ago, when I was in New York, Margaux had made a video of him, where he was supposed to pretend like he wasn't being looked at, but just carry on normally, and all that day he was surprised to remember how good it felt to act—and he knew without even seeing the tape that there was so much goodness in his acting—more than there would ever be in one of his paintings. Acting that day, he went on gloomily, had made him feel vital and happy, just as he had felt doing it so many years ago in high school.

SHEILA

So that's wonderful! To remember that . . .

SHOLEM

But don't you *see*? I have this terrible fear—it has always been my greatest fear—that my acting is better than my painting.

SHEILA

So what? If it is, then you can act.

SHOLEM

But Sheila, no! (*sighs*) Have you ever met Misha's uncle, Ezra? Well, he's a deeply opinionated man, and he's almost impossible to argue with. I remember once we were at a party, and he was talking about this teacher I had in art school who was a painter, who I really, really respected. He said, "You know, I find it really funny that someone who knows so much about painting, and who can talk so well about painting, and has such interesting ideas about painting—can't produce beautiful paintings."

SHEILA

And that chilled you? You felt that that was you?

SHOLEM

It's just—the moment he said that, I immediately recognized it as something I never wanted to be, and I immediately recognized it as something to avoid.

SHEILA

But . . . how can one avoid that?

SHOLEM

It's just . . . if I prayed, that is what I would pray for.

So Sholem went home and he prayed. He prayed that he would never become someone of whom it could be said: *It's funny he can talk so brilliantly about painting, but can't produce beautiful paintings*. And he continued, ever more rigorously, on the path he had started on. He did everything he could think of to make himself into the best painter possible. He worked night and day and thought only about paintings, and he painted and did nothing else.

And so it happened, slowly, over time, like the land erodes into the sea, that God wore down the beauty and worth of whatever he might have said about painting—dulled his thoughts' edges, blurred the vividness, precision, and confidence that once glittered in his every line—how he had once evoked things so simply, and with humor, too. His beautiful words became like silt at the bottom of the sea.

chapter 20

SHEILA'S FEAR

I had missed so many shifts at the salon without even calling in, and I felt too ashamed to tell them why. I couldn't
think of a good excuse. Uri had admired me as an employee;
now his image of me would be shot. The only way to keep
my dignity, it seemed, and my good name, was to quit. I
came up with an explanation of how I needed to focus on
finishing my play, that I had no extra time, that seeing Uri's
professionalism had taught me the most valuable lesson: I
must be as professional as him, but in *my* realm, not his. I
went to the salon with my resignation letter in hand. When
I arrived, I noticed a strange hush over the place; no one was
standing around gossiping, and the stylists avoided my eyes.
Even the receptionist, who always smiled and stopped what
she was doing to say hello, barely glanced up as I came in.
In the back room, I found one of the stylists, Amy, and

asked her the reason for the mood. She darted her eyes about, then spoke into the mirror that lined the pink walls. The stylists never looked each other in the eye; they only looked at each other in mirrors.

She said, "Uri announced that he's retiring and they're selling the salon. He'll still be working here part-time, but it seems Anthony believed that one day Uri would sell the salon to him. But of course Uri's not going to! When we found out this morning that he's selling it to Paul and Raoul, Anthony screamed before everyone and even the clients, *You're full of shit, Uri!* Then he punched his hand into the mirror and it shattered, and there was blood everywhere. Then Anthony packed up his scissors and left."

"Wow!"

"But we all know Anthony will be back tomorrow as though nothing ever happened."

I noticed Uri walking through the back room. Knowing I had few chances to approach him during the day, I went up quickly and handed him my resignation letter, which I had written the night before, so full of politeness and gratitude.

"Should I read this now?" he asked me. I nodded. I followed him into his office and stood there as he read one page, then flipped it and read the second one, then flipped it and read the third.

He said, "Well, we'll be sorry not to have you. You're an asset around here. But—if that's what you want to do . . ."

Then he grew distracted. "Did you hear what Anthony did?"

I nodded.

"He wanted me to sell him the salon—he said he always thought I would. But I never would! He has no consistency of character, no self-control. How could I trust him with the salon? He's not a loyal member of the team. He thinks only of himself. And you know he will never apologize for his outburst. What sort of man cannot apologize? But I have never heard Anthony admit that he's wrong." He shrugged. "I told Paul and Raoul to keep him on because I want to see how long a man can go without ever saying sorry."

Then Uri said, "Come, let me do your hair today. It is your last day, and I will put some highlights in."

"Thank you," I said, though I did not really want highlights. But I was moved by what a professional he was, to do me this final kindness, making himself, once again, into a man you could not criticize.

As I sat at his station, Uri worked on my hair, saying nothing. My letter was making me uneasy, and I began to wish I hadn't given it to him. I was starting to feel like I had made a mistake; it was incredibly stupid to leave the salon. I loved it there! And how would I make money now? It was so clear to me: the happiness I felt at the salon had been *real*, and I was giving it up out of some ill-considered vanity; the need to protect my image in Uri's eyes. As the moments passed, my decision became more irrevocable, and my life at the salon slipped farther away; I would soon have no place there at all. My panic increased as I tried to think of ways I could take my resignation back, meanwhile trying to remind myself that the point of life was not to avoid suffering—that every choice involved suffering—and that in choosing to leave the salon, I was choosing one kind of suffering, while choosing to stay would involve another, whereas going back and forth as I was doing now was the worst suffering of all, as it was an attempt to avoid life, which would leave me finally with nothing!

I sat like this, my brain going wild beneath Uri's hands, the cap bound tightly around my head, Uri plucking out strands of my hair. I suddenly saw: it was so ridiculously easy to end things! I had given him the letter, and before I could speak, my time there was over! My hair was being colored—then out the door for good. I had made a huge mistake!

I followed one of the girls to the bowl, and as she held my head and rinsed me off, the tension began rising in my neck. When she returned me to the chair to towel dry my head, I saw in the mirror what Uri had done: he had completely bleached out my hair! These were not highlights. The toner had turned my hair dry and gray—not a pretty soft white like Marilyn Monroe's or an Andy Warhol silver. It was an old woman's head. I looked like I was at the end of my life, and, worse, like the person who had lived *this* life. Uri returned and spread his hands wide, smiled at me, and said, "Well?"

I could not smile back. I felt like I had been erased, like no one would ever look at me again. But at least I had no inclination to glance into the mirror and tilt my head just so.

chapter 21

HOW GREAT IT IS TO BE
AN ADULT

When I was little, and I thought that children grew up and their parents grew down, so that one day the child became the parent and the parent became the child, I had in my head such an impressive idea of what an adult was. My father seemed to me to know everything. My mother had such assurance and command. Inside my head was a little square of awe, compact and complete.

They seemed as far away from me as a spaceship from the earth, orbiting in some darkness I could not comprehend. But now that I am an adult among adults, I am there. I am now here—in what once seemed like a stratosphere, another stratosphere entirely—but is this. This is the absolute outer limit of the human universe.

chapter 22

A STRANGER IS A FRIEND OF ANOTHER STRANGER ON ACCOUNT OF THEIR STRANGENESS ON EARTH

My mother had been calling for weeks, leaving messages on my phone, sending long and desperate emails, so that I finally felt: *Today is the day*. I would go and do what she needed me to do—clean up the trash in her basement, which was my entire life, and throw it all out, so she could proceed in her life with a clear mind.

I took the bus fifteen minutes north. When I arrived at her house she was not home, as I knew and expected she would not be. She was at work. I went down into the basement by myself. She had left garbage bags on the landing for me to clear everything away. The basement was different than in my memory—less a place filled with special meaning than just a place. But the air was reassuringly familiar: mildewy and warm.

I looked about to see where my mess was, but I couldn't find the mess. All the papers and books I had imagined cluttering everything up—there was nothing like that there. The hard brown carpet had recently been vacuumed, and there were two small hatboxes against the wall, one on top of the other.

I went up to the boxes and knelt and opened them, and in them was my stuff. *This* was the mess I had left behind? This was what had been cluttering my mother's mind for so long?

I glanced through the boxes, threw out some essays I knew I'd never want to read, and was left with a small stack of papers and pictures, plus a letter addressed to me, which had never been opened, and which I put in my pocket. I ascended from the basement with both boxes and went from her house. One box I put by the garbage bin outside. The other I carried home with me.

It was nine o'clock at night. I got on the southbound bus, passed beneath the bright fluorescents, and sat in the back. The air was humid. There were only three other people on the bus.

When the bus began to move, I pulled the envelope out of my pocket and turned it around. I didn't recognize the handwriting, and yet I did, a bit. Why hadn't I opened it before? I opened it now.

1. Dear Sheila,
2. On Sunday evening my son told me that you and he are separated. I was stunned by that news and am still having trouble believing it's true.
3. I thought you were soul mates, with so much in common and so able to help each other through life.
4. I think back to the spring when you told me that you were madly in love with him and that no one else made you feel that way.
5. I know he adores you as well and wants to take care of you. That kind of love is a rare gift.

1. It has been a very difficult year for both of you, with many unexpected stresses which have made life so hard.
2. But that is when we need each other most—just to know someone cares about you is so important.
3. There are few answers, I think, to many of our problems.
4. We just have to live through things.

1. That is how I am feeling with my husband now passed, and I have to believe and act as though it will get better.
2. Frustrating as life with him could be, my life is now quite empty without him.
3. He and I shared so many things, both good and bad, and had come to a place where we were able to appreciate what we had as being very special.

1. You have been such a part of my life and my family
   for the past few years, that it is hard to think of it
   without you.
2. I truly don't know what to say except that I am
   feeling very sad, as I think you are, too.
3. All my love, Odile.

I held the letter close, like a warm animal against my chest.

· *chapter 23* ·

BACK IN FRONT OF THE
BIKINI STORE

By the time I arrived home, I was thinking about Margaux. I just wanted to make her feel safe and good. If only I could figure out what would make her trust me, I would do it. So I really tried to think. There were two things I knew for sure about Margaux: she had never quit anything, and she felt she had too much empathy. So I hoped things could be saved. I hoped we could live through this.

But she had made a sacrifice for me, in letting herself be taped, while I had made no sacrifice for her. I had done nothing scary or of risk to myself for Margaux's sake. There was a real imbalance. But what could fix it? What did she need me to do? It would have to be something that would prove to her that I was *not* using her, that I would not leave her once I had taken from her what I thought she was useful for. But what could the sacrifice be? I considered it as I lay in my bed that night, and my dreams seemed to swirl in that direction. But when I woke the next morning, I had no idea what the gesture should be.

Only one person could help me.

Margaux and I sat on the stoop in front of the bikini store, and she looked down at her hands while I watched the people walk along Queen Street. She was breathing quietly and sitting very still. Then finally she looked at me and said, "I want you to finish your play."

"What! My embarrassing, impossible play!"

"Yes! And I want it to answer your question—about how a person should be—so that you never have to think about it anymore. So that whatever you do from that point on isn't about that question, and so our friendship won't be either. And you can use anything you need from me to answer that question—my words, whatever, just answer it."

It was the worst, most difficult thing she could have asked of me. And certainly she would be the only person left who could love me—I would have no new friends once my ugliness was out there in the world for everyone to see. I sat for a moment, sunk into my glumness. Her eyes drifted to my gray hair.

"And do it quickly," she said. "You're going to have to work harder than you've ever worked in your life."

I sat in silence, then turned to her.

"Does it have to be a play?"

She thought for a moment, then grinned. "No."

· *chapter 24* ·

THE CASTLE

I followed Margaux up the stairs to her apartment and into her studio. I was relieved to find a few paintings on the walls, freshly painted, just beginning. A computer had been moved into the space, and there were two old monitors on a desk, plus some pieces of paper taped to the walls— charts. She began telling me about a conversation she'd had a few weeks ago with her new gallerist in New York, who was putting her in a group show. I didn't know she was going to be showing in New York!

MARGAUX

(*excited*) I told him why I'm doing all the things I'm doing, and I talked a lot about my paintings, and I said that the less the work's about me, the more I get to use my life. It just felt like the healthiest conversation in the world!

SHEILA

What did he say?

MARGAUX

That I'm doing everything wrong! He asked if in Canada
people liked paintings small, and I said yes, and he said well
here in America we like our paintings big, and we don't
like them painted on wood, or when the paint is thin—

SHEILA

(*delighted*) He must have been so happy with you!

MARGAUX

Um, it's hard for me to say.

*Margaux turns to one of the charts on the wall and touches it gently.
Her voice gets quieter.*

You know, after you left my house that night, I kept quilting and thinking. I was up until dawn almost, and then I
knew it—what I needed to do to get rid of my bad feelings.
(*turning*) You know I never needed you to get rid of them
for me.

Sheila looks down.

The solution was not to speak *less* but to speak *more*, and not
through you, but through *myself*. That felt really right. But
what did I have to say? So I sat at my desk and began think-

ing of all the things I *have*, right? Like, I wanted to see what meaning there was between all the things around me. So I wrote down all my resources—all the things I have. For instance, I have Julia's mother's cottage, I have the Hamlet story, I have Sholem, I have four thousand dollars. I figured, you work from what you *have*. I wondered, *What would be the best outcome, taking everything I have?* So it really was about using variables and using the—what do you call them?—the invariables.

SHEILA

What do you mean, *invariables*?

MARGAUX

Well, it's like in life—you have the variables and you have the invariables, and you want to use them all, but you work around the invariables.

Margaux becomes quiet.

I thought *you* were an invariable—and then you left without saying a word.

SHEILA

You think of *me* as an invariable?

MARGAUX

Yes.

Then, very deep inside, something began to vibrate. I was an invariable. An *invariable*. No word had ever sounded to me more like love.

MARGAUX

So these past few weeks, I've been looking at everything I have—just sitting here looking, and it slowly became clear: it's a movie! I'm going to make a movie using everything I have! I'll sort of construct these scenes from everything I have, then when I'm done shooting, I'll put the scenes in some sort of instinctual order. I don't know what it's going to look like in the end, but I have faith that at the center of the film there'll be, like, this invisible castle, and each of the scenes will be like throwing sand on the castle. Wherever the sand touches, those different parts of the castle light up. At the end you'll have a sense of the entire castle. But you never actually *see* the entire castle.

SHEILA

Right.

MARGAUX

(smiles, relieved) You know, all week I was sitting at my computer, thinking, *Am I retarded? Am I retarded? Am I retarded?*

SHEILA

I understand the part where you say, "Am I retarded?"

. . .

Had anyone suggested at the time that it would not be the Egypt of the pharaohs that would survive and change the moral landscape of the world, but instead a group of Hebrew slaves, it would have seemed the ultimate absurdity.

chapter 25

ISRAEL BECKONS

Back at home, Sheila finds an email from Israel . . .

1. i have a hard-on right now in the vietnamese internet palace.
2. theres a guy next to me whos really getting into the porn. he just went to the bathroom and i think hes jacking off.
3. he just came back and yep, he smells like giz, hes kind of creepy, ex military or something, but the porn hes looking at looks pretty good.

1. so theres something i need done for me.
2. i want you to buy a porno mag, and i want you to look at that porno and get really horny thinking

about me fucking you like a dirty dog and cumming
hard down the back of your throat.

3. take the mag and roll it up tight. tape it so it doesnt
   move and put a condom over it. put some lube on
   your cunt and the mag.
4. spread your legs as far as you can and put the magcock
   up your cunt and fuck yourself.
5. then take pictures of you doing this and send them to
   me.

1. i know you once said that the idea of an old man
   fucking you in a portolet didnt turn you on but that
   wasnt the point.
2. the point was that it turned me on thinking you
   would do something like that for me.
3. its not the idea of you fucking a disgusting old man in
   a portolet that gets me going, no, i like the idea of
   you doing things i ask.
4. bye for now.

I saw there was no way of escaping a man like that. Even if
I went to the farthest shore, there would still be internet
access there and he would find me. Only if I never checked
my email, then I would be safe. But I *always* checked my
email, even when I tried not to. North Korea was the only
place I would be safe. But even there I would still have my
memories of him, so I would not be safe.

chapter 26

DESTINY IS THE SMASHING
OF THE IDOLS

I should have spent the night inside writing, figuring out how a person should be, like I meant to, but I was afraid. I wasn't ready. Instead I went out. I went to meet Israel. I went not knowing what would come. We agreed on a spot, at a bar on the longest street in the world. When I arrived on the corner, he was standing there smoking. He gave me a lazy look that cut at my heart and said, "Nice hair, old lady." We walked together to the bar, and he asked me if I had ever written him that letter from camp. I felt uneasy. I said no.

Inside the bar, I sat silently as he talked on about a coffee shop he wanted to open, while I just looked at his face. I couldn't believe he was a real person sitting there before me. He didn't ask me any questions. I wouldn't have known what to answer.

As we were finishing our second drink, he said, "Should we go?" So we left. I couldn't tell if I loved him or liked him or if I felt nothing at all. We got in a cab—his idea— and soon we were back at my apartment. I paid. We went into my bedroom, then I excused myself to use the bathroom. When I returned to the bedroom, he pulled off all my clothes. Then he took off his clothes. Looking at him, his belly was softer; his legs seemed stout. When he smiled, it did not make me feel special or strange. There was a vacancy in our touch, a deep well of nothing. Whatever bright thing had existed between us had left and moved on to other people. I made out with his penis until the moment came that he might fuck me. He was on top of me as I lay on my back. Then he hesitated and said, "Maybe I shouldn't."

"Okay."

I did not know why he said it, or if he would want to in ten minutes, or in the morning, or next week, or never again. We lay silently in my bed, and then my body felt it, deep and calm: what I wanted to do—something I had never done before. Without letting myself think about it a moment more, I shuffled down beneath the covers, say- ing to him as I did it, "I want to sleep beside your cock." I slithered down there and lay, my lips soft up against his dick. I felt his legs grow tense. "Get up," he said. "No." "Come up here," he said, more forcefully this time. But I knew that if I did, his desire for me might remain, and I wanted none of it left. I had to be so ugly that the humiliation I brought on myself would humiliate him, too. I would have to strip every last filament of gold from my skin—all the gold I had put there—and strip the gold from his skin, so that none of the gold on him would reflect onto me, and so none of the gold on me would reflect onto him, so we would be in utter darkness together. I curled myself around his legs. I knew he'd never understand why I was doing it—that he was misunderstanding what I meant. But I didn't care if he got me wrong. The way he saw me was not the same thing as me.

I felt so alert as I felt his dick shrink away, disgusted or ashamed. A few minutes passed. Then he turned his back on me. My nose went into his ass, and I felt its tiny hairs on my skin. A heat blanched my cheeks and my soul, but I remained there, stoic.

I had gone down, gone under, and when several minutes later I surfaced from beneath the hot, stuffy sheets, it felt truly like I was emerging into a new world entirely. Israel kept his back turned. We did not speak the rest of the night.

The next morning, I lay calmly on my side of the bed and watched as he stood in the middle of my room and dressed. After buttoning his shirt, he looked down into his shirt pocket and pulled out a quarter. He placed it on the windowsill beside my head with real deliberateness, then turned and walked away.

I glanced out the window, into the bright day.

What I had done in the night—it felt like the first choice I had ever made not in the hopes of being admired. I had not done it to please him. It was not to win someone's regard. Then, from inside of me came a real happiness, a clarity and an opening up, like I was floating upward to the heavens.

chapter 27

WHAT IS FREEDOM?

Say my first boyfriend was right. Say it's true that if I live the life that is truly inside me and extend my will into the world, I will wind up loveless, lost, and alone, my face in some stranger's hairy ass.

But if my fate is truly my fate, then trying to escape it by doing whatever I can to make my life resemble some more beautiful thing will only lead me more quickly to the place I most fear. If there can be no escape from who I am, then I ought to reach my end honestly, able to tell myself, at least, that I have lived it with all of my being, making choices and deciding, walking the whole way.

Who cares? If someone has to wind up, at the end of their long life, kneeling in a dumpster before a Nazi, it might as well be me. Why not? Aren't I human? Who am I to hold myself aloof from the terrible fates of the world? My life need be no less ugly than the rest.

ACT

4

· *chapter 1* ·

SHEILA THROWS HER SHIT

Now it was time to write. I went straight into my studio and thought about everything I had, all the trash and the shit inside me. And I started throwing the trash and throwing the shit, and the castle began to emerge.

I'd never before wanted to uncover all the molecules of shit that were such a part of my deepest being which, once released, would smell forever of the shit that I was, and which nothing—not exile, not fame—could ever disappear. But I threw the shit and the trash and the sand, and for years and years I just threw it. And I began to light up my soul with scenes.

I made what I could with what I had. And I finally became a real girl.

INTERMISSION

I was standing in line in the lobby of the theater, waiting to buy a soda at the bar, when I felt a tap on my shoulder. I turned around, and behind me was my husband, who I hadn't seen in half a year. He told me what he had been doing this last while, and I told him some of what I had doing since we'd seen each other last. Looking into his face, I felt the same tenderness I always felt with him, but which I began doubting the sufficiency and purity of as soon as we were married.

We moved gradually along the line toward the counter, and I felt inside of me a fluttering of love. There in the theater I had no doubt that it truly came from inside me—that it was meant for him, and that it truly was mine.

We had always talked easily and well, and as we carried

our drinks away, I asked him what he thought there was in us that forced us to tell stories to ourselves about our own lives—to make up stories that had such an arbitrary resemblance to our actual living. Why did we pick certain dots and connect them and not others? Why did we find it so irresistible to make ourselves into tragic figures with tragic flaws which were responsible for our pain? Maybe unfortunate things just happened; maybe there was just bad luck. Why did it seem like our greatest failures were caused by perversions in our souls?

"Perhaps it's evolutionary," he said. "If we saw ourselves in realistic proportions—how tiny we are, and how little ability we have to avoid the suffering that's an inevitable part of life—maybe we would be too discouraged to survive."

"Or maybe," I said, "the truth is so diffuse that our minds cannot even hold on to it."

We took our drinks and went outside to have a smoke, and I saw that he was carrying under his arm the next morning's newspaper. He was an editor at a daily. When we lived together, it had been so exciting to see him come home from the office with the paper, hot off the press, before its delivery to the street boxes. But that was a long time ago. For old time's sake, I smoked quietly as he read out the editorial to me, just like we used to do when we were married.

"It's written by a fourteen-year-old girl," he said, then cleared his throat.

When we are all in a culture together, we share a secret with each other, and this is true of every civilization down through time. Not even their art, not even their laws, their artifacts, their literature, their philosophies, their wars, their stone bowls can ever reveal that civilization's secret. Even today, with all we've built that will outlast us, we will not leave behind the secret that binds us. In this way, we are like any family at the core of which there is a secret that, even if someone asked, no one in that family— not even the snitchy, untrustworthy types—could ever reveal. In this way, we are all like a family together in the present, and no future civilization will ever know our secret—the secret of our existence together—just as we do not know the secrets that lived and died with the past.

He paused and looked up. "Huh. The headline on this is all wrong. I know because I wrote it. The foundry must have run out of the letters needed to make the word *Apocalypse*."

"What word did they use instead?" I asked.

He handed over the paper to show me. "*Plays*."

"*The World Fears Impending Plays?*"

"Yes. It's actually pretty good, no?"

"We-ll . . ." I hesitated. "I *do* think I've known some pretty powerful plays."

Then I thought about how plays had intermissions, because the audience grew tired. I wondered if I would ever get an intermission from the play my teenage boyfriend had written about me, which had somehow become my life. Or would the play end? If it really was a play, maybe it would. And for the first time ever I saw it: perhaps I was not fated to a life of loss and suffering—an end so degraded and mean.

Those had been *his* thoughts and fantasies. And that fourteen-year-old girl had managed to express a greater truth than my high school boyfriend ever had: that for all of our fears and all of our certainty, the bonds that unite us will remain a secret from us, always.

Then we heard a faint pinging, the signal that the final act was about to begin, and the lights inside the lobby flickered on and off, so, along with all the other smokers, we threw our cigarettes into the road and headed back inside.

ACT

5

THE UGLY PAINTING
COMPETITION

Sheila wakes to an email from Margaux . . .

1. i have been thinking: we're both unusually free people, but i think we have different mechanisms for being free.
2. with you, it's like you never believe you have any effect on people. maybe you don't think you're a person because you haven't decided what sort of person to be.
3. you always think no one can see you, which of course gives you the crazy freedom that lets you do whatever you want to.
4. for me, i always moved around a lot as a kid, so i never had any physical or recorded evidence of anything to do with the past. all my life i felt no restraint from anything in my past because it literally wasn't there.

5. when i was younger and i first started to be in the
   papers, no matter how small or mundane the media
   source, no matter how banal or positive the review
   was, i would see my name there and feel a weight of
   doom that would last about a week. it was just this
   mix of panic, depression, and anxiety that i couldn't
   escape or talk myself out of until it wore away.

1. i wanted you to know that i've started to find it
   interesting—this talking, this recording, this new freedom of letting my words be separate from my body.
2. i think growing up in a small town, what a bad
   person was, was to be the pretentious, rich, smirking
   artist in the corner of the room who no one understood, who was being intentionally obscure.
3. but maybe i don't need to be out there with this
   artist's statement about wanting to change society.
4. maybe we can be honest and transparent and give
   away nothing.

1. you know, when you first asked to tape me, it felt like
   you were saying, *can i take away your freedom?* and for a
   month i felt that same panic, depression, and anxiety
   that i used to feel when anyone wrote down my name.
2. but of course, i knew that the thing you most fear will
   always present itself, and what i feared most were my
   words floating separate from my body.
3. so i said okay to you, because for me the only way to
   go somewhere new is to do the thing i most fear.

4. i guess i have only ever solved my personal problems
    in uncomfortable ways.

*Margaux, Sholem, Misha, Jon, and Sheila gather in Jon and Sholem's
living room. The long-awaited Ugly Painting Competition has finally
arrived. Everyone sits on the couch or on chairs except for Sholem,
who stands before everyone.*

SHOLEM

Okay, here are the art school ground rules. The ground
rules are that the presentation has to—intentions are covered, the intention of the work is covered—we have to talk
about intentions and what we did and whether what we did
translated into what actually happened.

Laughter. Everyone starts speaking at once.

Don't stall this! Get going!
Wait!
Not at the same time!
Give us time to—

SHOLEM

The other thing that has to be discussed is whether you feel
you've succeeded in making an ugly painting. Okay, we'll
flip a coin: heads or tails?

MARGAUX

Tails.

I was going to say *tails* for you!
Who's got a coin?
Can I give you a check?
Here you go, here you go—

Sholem takes the coin from Jon.

SHOLEM

If it's tails, Margaux goes first.

Sholem flips.

Heads. I go first!

Sholem went and stood before us, and showed us the painting he had made by doing everything he hated when his students did it, and we agreed that it was truly ugly. There was nothing in it that could be called beautiful, nothing that made you want to look longer. Sholem sat down. Then it was Margaux's turn.

MARGAUX

Oh wow, the whole setup actually makes me nervous. Like, *Maybe it's not ugly enough!*

I'm so excited!
What's it called? What's it called?

MARGAUX

I have to tell you after you see it. Everyone close your eyes;
no cheating, close your eyes.

She turns the painting around.

Okay, ready!

Huge laughter.

What is it!!

MARGAUX

It's called *Woman Time*!

Ugliest title ever!
I love it!!
It's the funniest thing ever!

SHOLEM

You have to sit down; I put a chair there.

Margaux sits.

MARGAUX

It's fully art school.

MISHA

What's art school like?

MARGAUX

It's like . . . I don't know.

SHOLEM

First, what did you intend?

MARGAUX

Well, it's confusing, because *ugly*'s a confusing word for me, but—okay. What I really wanted to do, but I decided it was too conceptual and would probably lead to beauty, was to cover myself in paint and straddle the canvas and then have a rainbow coming out of a hole with a sunrise, and I was like, *It's great!—it's huge!—and it's so funny!* I wanted it to be four foot by five foot. Then I thought, *No*—'cause it was already in my head—*that's not right, I should follow my instincts more.* So I thought, *I'll just do it instinctually,* and the same thing came out!

SHEILA

Why four foot by five foot?

JON

It makes no sense.

MARGAUX

It's an ugly size.

SHOLEM

I think three foot by four foot is an ugly size. It's into the larger-than-normal.

MISHA

Can you explain to me, because I've never been to art school, why the painting is not ugly-great, it's just ugly-ugly?

MARGAUX

Well, it's confusing 'cause I like ugly a lot of the time, so I tried to think of an ugly I didn't like or that actually felt slightly repulsive.

SHEILA

So you think your instinct is so beautiful that it had to be counterintuitive?

MARGAUX

Well, everything I like is ugly-beautiful. For me, what's truly ugly is, like, tight blue jeans with cowboy boots and a lot of makeup—restrained things. That's really ugly—or like a really detailed drawing of a rocking horse. I think anything tight is truly ugly for me. Not ugly for the world— people love that—but it just looks awful to me. It looks like death.

SHOLEM

Was there anything along the way, sort of from beginning to end, that didn't go according to plan?

MARGAUX

I had no plan.

MISHA

Was there anything that surprised you?

MARGAUX

I started making a movie, and then I painted this, and then I went back to painting, and now I paint differently!

SHOLEM

Really? How?

MARGAUX

I don't know . . .

JON

I have a question: Would you care if this was thrown in the garbage?

MARGAUX

No.

SHEILA

I like it! I want to hang it in my kitchen.

MARGAUX

You can have it!

SHEILA

How did you know when to stop? You know what I mean?

MARGAUX

Oh! I think I had to really resist fixing things. You know?

SHEILA

Do you find the colors ugly?

MARGAUX

(*tired*) I don't know. I looked at all my colors, and my instincts were like: black and yellow, black and yellow. It was very quick, you know. Like: *I should smoothly blend an orange ball.* Misha saw this, and Misha was like, "I actually pictured orange circles on white background!"

Everyone laughs.

I mean, it's just such a default, the abstract, 'cause you're going with your instincts, but it *was* abstract, and then it became a vagina.

Sholem stands and approaches the painting.

SHOLEM

Well, I think my suspicions were largely correct. The colors are ugly. Yellow and black is, like, textbook ugly, and the way that shape on the lower right-hand side is almost

like a thumb. I find that so *hideously* ugly. And I find the
drip ugly, because nothing upsets me more than seeing a
drip. It's like this gross shorthand for expression—

MARGAUX

I like this critique! This is awesome!

SHOLEM

But see, the saving grace is your touch. The nonugly is your
touch. I knew it would be like this! The way this line sort
of whorls in on itself, and you have these two beautiful
streaks of this gorgeous red—

MARGAUX

I knew he was going to like that! I was like, *I should go fix
that!*

SHOLEM

—and the way it sits on that gorgeous sort of crimson-
orange ground. Again, so special. Your touch is all over
this painting. Your snaky, searching line is everywhere.
And that's one of the greatest strengths of your paintings. You haven't obliterated your hand. Even though
you said you wanted to make this really awful thing, your
strength is still in there. Your mark is there in everything
you do!

MARGAUX

(*laughing*) I've never been more flattered in my whole entire life!

SHEILA

If somehow it ended up in a group show with your name attached to it, would you be embarrassed?

MARGAUX

No. I could hang this in a show if I wrote, *Ugly Painting Competition with Sholem.* I wouldn't mind. But I don't want to compromise my own work. So my work can be about my own life sometimes, but I would have to be thoughtful, and in this case that would mean titling it that way.

SHEILA

Would you show this at the Katharine Mulherin Gallery? If she came to your studio and was like, *Margaux, I love this new direction*?

MARGAUX

She does that all the time, and I'm like, *That's not done!*

Sheila smiles.

I walked home alone. There was always a fear in me of what choice would make me less human, that a lapse could be like a pink eraser and smudge me. I felt my life was under the hand of an art student—a ruthless, Nietzschean art student. I tried to be the mark that could lead such a hand to draw a picture of a real human. Together the hand and I would live, have no experiences that weren't human. Then I heard news of a seed whispering, *Everything that happens to man conforms to the well-worn patterns of humanity.*

chapter 2

THE SACK

In a few hours it would be Margaux's birthday; it was time to deliver the champagne I had promised I would take to her studio so long ago, when I had missed her birthday and we were first becoming friends. I took the bottle from the refrigerator, went down the stairs, and set off into the street. When I arrived at Margaux's place, she opened the door to me, and she smiled. We went up the stairs, straight into her studio, which smelled of grease and paint, then we sat on the floor and drank the champagne from her very best cups.

We spoke for several hours, getting happier and more drunk. Then Margaux walked me to my apartment, since it was always so hard for us to leave each other, and we stood together in my garden, and the breezy air blew all around us. The clean scent of pine trees was up, and it mixed with the sweet stink of garbage bags that the neighbors had left out for pickup.

I listened as Margaux finished the story she had been telling me, about the girl she had been in art school with—the one who had left to join a Buddhist colony to paint pretty colors on the insides of temples. Shortly before her friend left, they had sat together in one of the classrooms, after dark, cross-legged on a table. The girl wanted to tell Margaux about Margaux's other lives, and she pulled Margaux's hands into her own and reverently closed her eyes. Margaux was dubious but willing. A few moments passed between them in silence, then the girl opened her eyes suddenly and said, "I had a vision. There is a person walking through a busy marketplace in some other faraway land. She is carrying a sack with something really heavy in it. The sack is really heavy. So she throws away the sack." The girl's brown eyes filled with pity, and she gripped Margaux's hands. "She didn't know how valuable the thing was inside."

Margaux burst into tears upon hearing this, and her eyes filled with tears to remember it. "Do you still like me, even though I'm crying?" She laughed.

I smiled and nodded.

"All this time you've been recording me . . . you have been *looking* at me, really *looking*!" It was like she was seeing it for the first time, and her eyes got wide. "I wonder if it's true that . . . Well, a person wouldn't spend all her time looking at something that doesn't have value, right?"

I nodded very gently.

She recovered herself and blew out a big breath that threw

up her bangs. Then she returned to being the quarterback and slapped me on my arm. I watched as she was about to leave the garden, but before she was past the fence, she turned and walked back to where I was standing, and said into my ear, "I have never had a kinder friend . . . or a more difficult one."

As Margaux walked away, I thought about what I wanted to do. I would do it, too. I knew the value of what was in that sack. I would carry that sack and never put it down. I would carry it to the end.

Now I was tired. All I wanted was to rest. The six days of Creation each have their own morning and evening, thereby showing their beginning and end. Only the seventh day has neither morning nor evening. It stands outside of Creation, belonging to the divine order alone.

I wanted a day without morning or evening. I wanted a day of rest.

A star shone brightly down into my garden, poking behind the clouds. And I stared up at the night sky. There were all those stars with nothing around them, protecting them. They were up there and I was down here, and into my head came the idea of fences; how when you have something you value, the next thing you have to do is build a fence around it. As it has been said, *Tithes are a fence for wealth. Vows are a fence for abstinence. Silence is a fence for wisdom.* These fences do not protect what we value from other people, like those fences that prevent things from being stolen away. These are fences against our own selves; against what in our selves can chase what we value away. I told myself, *Catalog what you value, then put a fence around these things*. Once you have put a fence around something, you know it is something you value. Put a fence around what you want to make holy, and crown it with the seventh day. Crown it with rest. The fence and the rest make it holy.

I *did* value Margaux, but only now did I understand something I had not before: Margaux was not like the stars in the sky. There was only one Margaux—not Margauxs scattered everywhere, all throughout the darkness. If there was only one of her, there was not going to be a second one. Yet in some strange way, somewhere inside me, I had always believed that if I lost Margaux, I could go out and find another Margaux.

Now it seemed so horrible to me. And didn't it explain everything? But I had never wanted to be one person, or even believed that I was one, so I had never considered the true singularity of anyone else. I said to myself, *You are only given one*. The one you are given is the one to put a fence around. Life is not a harvest. Just because you have an apple doesn't mean you have an orchard. You have an apple. Put a fence around it. Once you have put a fence around everything you value, then you have the total circle of your heart.

chapter 3

THE GRAVEDIGGER

There lived a man in our town who labored up at the Mount Pleasant Cemetery. Those who worked with him consider him a loyal man, solid and unshakable. When he was young, he had been a wanderer through many of the great cities of the world, but after seeing what was what, he made some choices and began to apply the run-of-the-mill gifts the gods had given him to what he determined with his own mind was important. He took the job as a grave-digger, and three decades later, he worked there still.

One morning, a ditchdigger, who was no longer young but believed himself so, hurried through the cemetery, late for work as usual. He ran past the gravedigger, who had been up and digging for several hours already. The grave-digger nodded hello.

The ditchdigger nodded back and, out of breath, paused

to take a moment's rest. He pulled out a cigarette and lit it. For a few moments he watched the gravedigger work, then he said, uneasily, "Are you sure you should be digging there? Over there the sun is brighter—wouldn't it make for a nicer plot over by those trees?"

The gravedigger looked to where the man was pointing. He could see why the man would say that, but he knew from experience that it was not always best to be in the sun or beside a grove of trees. There were advantages and disadvantages. Who could say which plot was best—this one or that one or a third?

"Right here is fine," the gravedigger said. "It's not the plot, it's the grave."

The man shook his head and laughed. "If I had your job, I'd always be asking myself which plot was best. I'd keep on switching! You'd have this whole land covered in small holes, two feet deep."

The gravedigger nodded and smiled gently, imagining the scene—all those bodies piling up by the gates. He might have been this way too, but long ago he realized his intelligence didn't extend so far—to know what was good from what was best—so he taught himself to dig well, and did.

The man continued to watch the gravedigger work. When the gravedigger dumped the soil, it barely made a sound. When he cut into the ground with the shovel, it went in so neatly. Why was he doing this so carefully—in the isolation of the cemetery! Who was he performing for?

"Come on!" the ditchdigger cried suddenly, impatient, feeling like the world was passing them by. "Why the care!

You're only going to fill it up this afternoon—and then it's going to be swimming with maggots and worms."

The gravedigger stopped his work to reply, but the man had already set off in the direction of his job, loping between the headstones, now very far away.

The gravedigger said to himself, alone, "Not everyone can be a gravedigger. You have to make a neat job of it. I met a man once. He dug ditches. He wanted to see a grave. He was impressed when he saw me digging this way, how straight and deep it was. I told him: *It has to be. A human body is going in this grave.*"

THE GODS

A few weeks later, Sholem knocked on my door. He told me that he had been feeling uneasy. Though we'd held the Ugly Painting Competition, no winner had been declared. I admitted that this had kind of been bothering me too. We had simply never discussed it: Was the winner of an Ugly Painting Competition the person who made the uglier painting, as Sholem had, or was it the person who, though trying just as hard, made a painting that was inadvertently beautiful? Sholem said that he and Margaux had talked about it, and they'd come up with an idea that seemed fair. They would compete in a squash game. If Margaux won, then the person who made the more beautiful painting would be considered the winner of the competition, and if Sholem won, it would be the person whose painting was actually uglier. Did I want to come with them and see? Of course I did! I was really eager to know who would win.

The following afternoon, we gathered in our gym outfits, but while Margaux and Sholem went straight for the courts, Misha and Jon and I went up to the observation deck and arranged ourselves along the concrete wall, resting our arms along its edge, peering down into the court below. The squash court's white walls narrowed in a severe fore-shortening, making it look like a fluted, funnel-shaped room. The tan lacquered wood of the court's floor gleamed up at us, and I could see the stroke marks left behind by the players who'd worn dark-soled shoes.

We didn't speak, just waited. The stuffy, sweaty smell of the gym hung in the air behind us. Then we saw Margaux's blond head and dark roots from above as she walked onto the court—and Sholem's curly black hair, his skinniness and bare legs, following behind.

We waited, drinking from our water bottles, silent. Then they began. The game went very slowly at first, then grew more and more focused. Soon Margaux and Sholem were running back and forth, breathing very heavily. They smacked the ball against the wall, dodged into each other's part of the court, and slammed against the back wall, groaning. They nodded briefly when the other made a good move. They rubbed sweat from their brows and hit the ball too high. They ran forward and bent low, and at one point Sholem threw himself to the ground. Margaux followed the rolling ball, walking very slowly, and tossed it to Sholem to serve. He smacked it high in the air and ran to the edge of the court and missed.

After about half an hour of this, I heard Misha say to Jon, "Do you know the score?" Jon looked at me blankly, then we both looked at Misha. I told them I had no idea.

So we turned our attention more intently to the game. We watched and listened with real concentration, but none of us could hear anything from below except for explosions of laughter, moans, and cursing, and Sholem saying, "Fuck! I hate this fucking game!"

We remained very still, and we watched. Then finally Jon said, in his sweetly caustic drawl, "I don't think they even know the rules. I think they're just slamming the ball around."

And so they were.

ABOUT THE AUTHOR

SHEILA HETI is a writer who lives in Toronto.